WINNING HANNAH'S HEART

"One minute to midnight!" Wyatt called.

Hannah stepped beneath the mistletoe, heart pounding as her two best buddies, Carter and Luke, made their way toward her—one with his easy swagger, the other with his quiet smile, both vying for the opportunity to be her first kiss of the new year.

Ben Landry stood at the counter, handing his card to Wyatt, that gray Stetson shadowing his eyes and deepening the dimple in his cheek. He leaned in, his warm voice brushing her ear. "Happy New Year, Hannah."

Hannah caught a hint of his leather and spice cologne. What would it be like to have *this man*, with his soft voice and adorable dimple, waiting for her kiss under the mistletoe?

"Two! One!"

Confetti burst. The room erupted. And Hannah turned—not toward Carter or Luke, but toward Ben—and kissed him.

BOOK 3

Winning Hannah's Heart

JoAnn Charles

Prairieland Press

Prairieland Press
PO Box 2404
Fremont, NE 68026-2404
Printed in the U.S.A.

Cover Design by Prairieland Press
Book Design by Prairieland Press

eBook ISBN-13: 978-1-944132-56-9
Paperback ISBN-13: 978-1-944132-57-6
Hardcover ISBN-13: 978-1-944132-58-3

Prairieland Press

For Larry, who always supports my dreams,
and for Mom and Dad, Always!

One

HANNAH

HANNAH MITCHELL SAT in her car and stared at the front door of the Rusty Spur. Her fingers picked at the sequins on her silver clutch. She'd promised Alyssa she'd come to Wyatt's New Year's Eve party at the Spur, and they'd even gone shopping together in Kearney just for the occasion: new dresses, new shoes, new eye shadows to match. But now that she was actually here, her courage was dissolving faster than sugar in hot coffee.

New Year's Eve at the Rusty Spur meant couples everywhere, slow dancing and stealing kisses, counting down to midnight with someone who mattered. And Hannah would be the awkward third wheel, watching it all from the sidelines. Again.

She'd never really minded being single before. Through her twenties, she'd been perfectly content with her independence, her friendships, her life in Bluestem. But turning thirty last month had shifted something inside her. Suddenly, watching her friends pair off made her feel like she'd blinked, and missed a train everyone else had managed to catch.

She squeezed the steering wheel one last time, a silent command for courage, and pushed open her car door. As she picked her way across the icy parking lot, she wished she'd worn boots instead of heels. Or better yet, never promised Alyssa she'd be here. Then she could have stayed home and watched the ball drop from her living room couch without a guilty conscience.

A wave of warmth and noise hit her as she stepped inside. The Rusty Spur was decked out for the holiday: colored lights zigzagged across the ceiling, and the air was thick with the mingled scents of barbecue, beer, and someone's questionable body spray. Country music blared from the speakers, competing with the laughter and chatter of what looked like half the town of Bluestem.

At the far end of the room, she spotted LeAnne Hudson. The innkeeper's auburn hair was swept back with a sparkly headband, her green velvet dress looking like it belonged on a Currier and Ives Christmas card. But it wasn't LeAnne or her festive outfit that made Hannah freeze. It was the stranger sitting across from her. He looked like the answer to the definition of "tall, dark, and handsome." If someone had asked her, Hannah would have just pointed across the room and said, "Yep. There he is. That's what it looks like!"

LeAnne caught her gaze and waved, signaling for her to join them. Hannah straightened her shoulders and managed what she hoped was a casual smile as she nodded and waved back. She took a step toward LeAnne and her mystery man when a voice stopped her.

"Hannah, Sweetheart! Can you come and help me? Just for a moment?"

She turned to see Mrs. K. waving at her from behind a table piled high with snacks. Even though Mrs. K.'s son Wyatt and her husband Dale technically owned the bar and grill, Mrs. K.

ran the show when it came to the food, decorating, and hospitality.

Hannah hesitated, glancing back toward LeAnne's booth. Tall-dark-and-handsome was leaning in, saying something that made LeAnne laugh. The moment was clearly private.

Mrs. K. waved again with more urgency. Hannah sighed and made her way to the snack table.

"Oh, honey, you look beautiful! That dress is perfect on you."

The simple compliment sent a wave of warmth through her. "Thank you, Mrs. K. You look lovely too." And she did—her silver hair was styled in soft curls, and her burgundy blouse sparkled with tiny beads that caught the light. "What do you need help with?"

"Could you put those pinwheels on a platter? They're disappearing faster than I can refill the tray."

Hannah set her clutch down and got to work, arranging ham and cream-cheese pinwheels in neat circles. She welcomed the busywork. If she focused on making the food perfect, she wouldn't have to think about midnight, or the handsome stranger at LeAnne's table, or how turning thirty had suddenly made her acutely aware of the empty space in her life.

"Hannah? You still here?" Mrs. K. appeared at her elbow, holding a tray of mini tacos. "I didn't mean for you to spend your entire evening working at the snack table. It's time for you to have some fun." Mrs. K. lowered her voice to a stage whisper. "You know, the room is full of single, good-looking men tonight. Even more than usual."

Hannah managed a polite laugh. "Are you looking for a man, Mrs. K.?"

Mrs. K. chuckled, her laugh warm as cocoa. "You know I've been happily married since 1989. But that dress isn't meant for kitchen duty. Go find your friends and enjoy yourself. It's New Year's Eve!"

Before Hannah could come up with an excuse, Alyssa swooped in, hugging her so hard the platter of pinwheels nearly toppled. Alyssa's boyfriend Riley followed behind her, smiling at the two of them.

"There you are! I thought you'd never get here," Alyssa said, still clutching Hannah.

"Fashionably late, as always," Hannah said, hugging her back.

"Happy New Year, Hannah," Riley said, offering a quick hug of his own. "Alyssa's been watching the door for you all night. She was afraid you'd decided to bail on us."

"Not a chance," Hannah said, accepting his quick hug. "Someone has to keep you two from getting too sappy."

"Impossible," Riley said, and Alyssa flashed him a crooked smile that somehow made Hannah feel both happy and utterly miserable, all at the same time.

Alyssa tugged her toward their table. "Riley and I saved you a seat."

They settled in at a round table where Riley's sister Kate and her date were already sharing a plate of loaded potato skins. Hannah slid into the empty chair between Alyssa and Kate.

For a few moments, she let herself relax, soaking in the comfort of her friends and the hum of the party. But when the DJ switched to a line dance, Hannah decided she'd spent enough time at the couples' table. "I love this song!" she said, maybe a little louder than necessary, and dashed to the dance floor.

For a few glorious minutes, she didn't have to think about being the odd one out or about turning thirty without someone special in her life. She was just Hannah Mitchell, enjoying the music, spinning and laughing beneath the colored lights. But as soon as the song ended, the DJ put on a slow tune, and the spell was broken.

As couples paired off around her, Hannah spotted Carter Manchester and Luke Merriwether at the pool table. Although Carter was a few years older than she and Luke, the three of them were among the last of their childhood friends who still called Bluestem home. As the years passed and classmates drifted away, they'd only grown closer—more like siblings than anything else.

Hannah sauntered over and perched on a barstool. "Evening, Boys."

Carter looked up from the pool table, mouth curved in that cocky, boyish grin that was as much a part of him as his sandy hair and broad shoulders. "Well, well, well. Cue the fireworks. Look who's finally here."

Luke set down his pool cue and leaned against the table, his grin widening to match Carter's. "You clean up nice, Hannah Banana."

"I try," Hannah said, smoothing down her

silver dress. She nodded at the pool table. "Who's winning?"

"I am," Carter and Luke said in unison, then glared at each other.

Hannah laughed, the sound bubbling up from somewhere genuine inside her. These two could always do that—pull her out of her own head when she was spiraling. She settled onto her stool, feeling the knot in her shoulders loosen.

"Word to the wise," Carter said, aiming his pool cue at the ceiling. "Watch where you're walking. Mrs. K. went all out with the mistletoe this year."

Hannah followed Carter's cue upward to the little green traps waiting to catch unsuspecting partygoers.

"She's practically turned this place into a mistletoe minefield," Luke said, chalking his cue. "A guy can't walk to the bathroom without risking an awkward encounter."

"Speak for yourself," Carter said, a sly grin on his face. "I consider it a target-rich environment."

Hannah laughed. "Of course you do. Which answers the question why Carter is flying solo tonight. But what about you, Merriwether. I thought sure you'd have a date."

Luke glanced up from studying the table. "I thought so, too."

"Oh?"

"She cancelled a couple of hours ago." He leaned over and sank the nine ball with an easy stroke.

"Ouch. What happened?"

"Emergency appendectomy in Valentine." Luke straightened and moved around the table, examining his next shot. "She's a surgical nurse. Duty called."

"That's dedication," Hannah said.

"That's dating a nurse on New Year's Eve." Luke's tone was light, but Hannah caught the slight shrug of disappointment in his shoulders.

Carter missed his shot, the eight ball rolling harmlessly past the corner pocket. He straightened up and fixed those mischievous blue eyes on her. "So tell me, Hannah Mitchell—who's going to be the lucky guy standing with *you* under the mistletoe at midnight? Who gets to be your first kiss of the brand new year?"

A flush crept up her cheeks. The question stung more than it should have. "Those who plan ahead make sure they're safely in the ladies' room at midnight."

"Now that would be a tragedy," Luke said, aiming his cue with exaggerated care. "Especially since I've just been named the official midnight kisser of the Rusty Spur."

Carter raised an eyebrow. "Named by who? Yourself?"

"By process of elimination," Luke said. "Riley's taken, Wyatt's busy, and you, Carter, wouldn't know how to kiss a woman if she came with instructions."

Hannah burst out laughing despite herself. Luke was usually so serious, but something about competing with Carter always brought out his mischievous side.

Carter scoffed. "I don't think Hannah wants to be kissed by a man who spends his days with his hands up a cow's—"

"Carter!" Hannah cut him off, laughing.

He held up his hands. "I was going to say business end." He winked at her. "The point is, the good doctor here doesn't have nearly the experience I do when it comes to kissing beautiful women."

"Experience doesn't equal skill," Luke said,

sinking his shot with a satisfying thunk. "Game over, Cowboy." Luke turned to Hannah with an exaggerated bow. "Now, Hannah, about that midnight kiss…we can show Carter here how it's done."

Carter set down his cue and crossed his arms. "Hold on. Hannah's known me longer. I'm the one who drove her to the emergency room when she broke her wrist falling off that horse. Remember, Hannah? I held your hand through the entire operation."

"Operation?" Hannah said, laughing. "I was thirteen and they set my arm in a cast. Hardly an operation."

"Hannah, remember sophomore year? Biology? Lab partner for the entire year?" Luke asked. "That's got to count for something. Way more than one measly visit to the emergency room with some kid who had just scored his drivers' license."

Hannah shook her head, fighting back another laugh. These two were ridiculous, but their banter was exactly what she needed tonight. No awkward silences, no pitying looks, just easy friendship and harmless flirtation—the kind that meant absolutely nothing and they all knew it.

"Well, let's see. Carter has the Manchester family charm—"

Carter gave a deep bow. "Thank you."

"But Luke has those gentle hands that have saved...what, a million animals?"

Luke waggled his eyebrows. "Very gentle hands."

"Manchester charm or Merriwether gentleness..." Hannah tapped her chin, pretending to ponder. "That's a tough call. I need time to think it over." She grabbed her clutch and slid off her stool, ignoring Carter and Luke's groans of protest.

She couldn't help it; a laugh bubbled up at their ridiculousness. With a slight lift of her brow, she pointed at the drooping sprig of mistletoe hung over the bar. "All right, gentlemen. Meet me under the mistletoe at midnight," she said, her smile widening, "and we'll see who the lucky winner is."

Two

HANNAH

HANNAH SLIPPED AWAY from the pool table just as Carter and Luke's ridiculous debate about who was most deserving of her midnight kiss reached a fever pitch. She sneaked a glance over her shoulder.

Luke grinned, Carter winked, and Hannah laughed, wondering how she'd gotten herself into this mess. Maybe she should slip away to the ladies' room at midnight after all. That would be the simplest solution.

She made her way toward the bar. A glass of wine might help clear her head. Or cloud it further. Either way, it would give her something to do with her hands besides fidget with her clutch.

As she weaved through the crowd toward the bar, her gaze found LeAnne's table again. Once again, LeAnne smiled and motioned for her to join them.

Hannah hesitated only a moment before changing course. The wine could wait. Her curiosity about tall-dark-and-handsome couldn't. If he was LeAnne's date, she'd simply make polite conversation and move on. But if he wasn't... how many handsome strangers passed through Bluestem? And on New Year's Eve, of all nights?

Hannah smoothed her dress and made her way toward LeAnne's table. A nervous energy thrummed beneath the surface as she approached, which was ridiculous. She was just being friendly, after all.

The stranger sat with his back to her. Broad shoulders filled out his suit jacket, and dark hair curled slightly at the nape of his neck, just a touch too long for a typical businessman. A gray Stetson rested on the table next to him.

Hannah smiled at the sight of it and felt herself relax. Cowboys she could talk to—it was practically the language of Bluestem. He might be dressed nicer than most of the men at the

Rusty Spur tonight, but that Stetson told her everything she needed to know.

She straightened her shoulders and approached the table with newfound confidence. "LeAnne! Happy New Year!"

"Hannah! I'm so glad you stopped by. We were just talking about you."

Hannah blinked, her steps faltering. *Talking about me? Why?*

The stranger turned, and Hannah's breath caught. Up close, he was even more striking than she imagined—warm brown eyes, a square jaw, and a dimple in his left cheek that should have come with a warning label.

"You haven't met Ben yet, have you?" LeAnne asked. "He's renting a room at the Whitemore while he's here for the next few months."

"Hello, Hannah," the man said, extending his arm. His warm smile made his eyes crinkle at the corners and his dimple deepen. "Ben Landry. It's nice to finally meet you. I've heard a lot about you."

His grip was firm but gentle, and something about the warmth of his palm against hers sent a small thrill up her arm.

"We were just talking about the church's

winter festival," LeAnne said. "You're the chairman this year, right?"

Hannah grimaced slightly. "I guess so. I just couldn't stand the thought of it being cancelled. So I told Pastor John, 'Sure, I can do that'. By the time I came to my senses, it was too late to back out."

Ben laughed. "I know exactly what you mean. I've had my share of 'what did I just volunteer for?' moments."

Before Hannah could respond, a large hand landed on her shoulder.

"Sorry to interrupt, folks," Luke said, his voice smooth as honey, "but Wyatt says we need more dancers on the floor! And I need a partner—so I'm stealing Hannah away."

Hannah's startled gaze looked up at Luke. "Now? But I just sat down."

Luke squeezed her shoulder. "Come on, Hannah Banana. You promised me a dance. Remember?"

Had she? Hannah couldn't remember making any such promise. But it was possible. She had a tendency to do those sorts of things.

"Sorry to dash off," she said, smiling apologetically at LeAnne and Ben, "but a promise is a promise. It was nice to meet you, Ben. I'm sure I'll see you again soon."

Ben nodded. "I'm counting on it."

Luke held her hand as he guided her through the crowd. "So, who's the guy?"

"Ben Landry," Hannah said, letting Luke spin her onto the dance floor. "He's renting a room at the Whitemore. That's all I could find out before you whisked me away. Seems nice."

"You think so, huh?" Luke dipped her dramatically, and Hannah wondered if Luke had entered them into some dance contest she knew nothing about.

"Hey!" Hannah said, trying to keep her balance as Luke led her through another spin. "Could we maybe tone down the *Dancing with the Stars* routine? I'm wearing heels, you know."

Luke grinned and slowed his steps, settling into a more reasonable rhythm. "Okay. If you say so. Now, about that midnight kiss . . ."

"Midnight isn't for another two hours, Luke. I'm still considering my—"

Before she could finish, Carter appeared, grinning like he'd been waiting for this exact moment to cut in. "My turn," he said, reaching for her hand.

Before Hannah could process what was happening, Luke twirled her into Carter's arms, as smoothly as if they'd practiced it.

She lost track of time after that, caught up in a whirl of music and laughter and their playful tug-of-war. If Carter claimed her for a slow song, Luke would swoop in for the next one. When Luke brought her a plate of cheese and crackers, Carter handed her a plastic cup of sparkling cider.

For the first time in months, she wasn't on the sidelines or counting minutes until she could leave. She was right in the thick of things, laughing so hard her ribs hurt, grateful for these two ridiculous men who knew exactly how to rescue her from herself.

"Fifteen minutes to midnight, folks!" Wyatt called, his voice booming over the speakers. "Find your special someone!"

Mrs. K. worked her way through the crowd, passing out cardboard hats and cheap noisemakers.

"I believe we have a date, Ms. Mitchell," Luke said, sliding up beside her.

"Actually, I think that date is with me," Carter said, appearing on her other side, tipping his cowboy hat toward her. "The lady promised to meet the better man under the mistletoe, and we all know who that is."

Hannah's stomach dropped. She'd been having so much fun, she'd almost forgotten about that promise. Almost.

"Ten minutes, everyone!"

Hannah pointed toward the cluster of mistletoe hanging above the polished oak bar. "Meet you both there at midnight. As promised."

Before either man could answer, she slipped away into the crowd. She needed time to think. It was just a kiss, she told herself. A checked box on the New Year's Eve bingo card. With one of her best friends.

But which one?

As the seconds ticked closer to midnight, her heart beat louder; her decision felt heavier. For a wild moment, she considered disappearing; following her first instinct and locking herself in the bathroom with the sound of the countdown muffled through the door.

But she'd promised Carter and Luke she'd choose a winner at midnight. And a promise was a promise. Hannah headed for the bar and that large sprig of mistletoe that seemed to grow bigger with each step she took.

Ben Landry was at the counter, handing his credit card to Wyatt. His gray Stetson hat cast a shadow across his eyes, which somehow made his dimple more noticeable. It suited him perfectly, and Hannah's stomach did that fluttery thing again.

He looked up as Hannah approached, the surprise on his face quickly replaced by a warm smile. "Taking a break from your fan club?" he asked, nodding toward Carter and Luke, who were making their way through the crowd toward them.

She couldn't help but smile. "They have been a bit outrageous tonight, haven't they!"

Ben nodded. "A little. But it looked like the three of you were having a good time. The perfect way to ring in the New Year."

"I guess," Hannah said. And she had been having a good time. Up until now. Up until the time when she actually had to make a choice between them.

"One minute!" Wyatt's voice rang out over the growing excitement of the crowd.

Hannah forced herself to turn her back on

Ben. She stepped beneath the mistletoe, staring at the two men walking toward her.

"Ten! Nine! Eight!"

Carter: protective, gallant, and too good-looking for his own good.

"Seven! Six! Five!"

Luke: attentive, caring, with a dry wit that always caught her off guard.

"Four! Three!"

Ben leaned in, and his voice brushed her ear. "Happy New Year, Hannah."

Hannah caught a hint of his leather and spice cologne. What would it be like to have *this man*, with his soft voice and adorable dimple, waiting for her kiss under the mistletoe?

"Two! One!"

Confetti burst. The room erupted. And Hannah turned—not toward Carter or Luke, but toward Ben—and kissed him.

For one heart-stopping moment, Ben's lips froze against hers. She could sense his hesitancy and surprise before his hand found her waist, steadying her as the crowd jostled around them.

The kiss lasted only seconds before Hannah pulled away, her cheeks burning. The count-down cheers faded into the background as she stared into Ben's startled face. His dimpled smile had disappeared, replaced by an expression of complete bewilderment.

Shame prickled up her neck and straight into her ears. She stumbled back, nearly crashing into someone behind her.

"Oh gosh, I—I'm sorry." Her voice sounded thin and too loud, and her face was on fire. "I don't know why I— I mean, I do know, but—" Words tangled up in her mouth, coming out in a rush. "I shouldn't have just— I should have asked—"

All around them, the celebration continued. Couples kissed. Friends hugged. Glasses clinked together. No one seemed to notice her moment of insanity; no one except Ben, Carter, and Luke, all frozen with matching looks of shock. "I need to go," she said, not sure Ben could even hear her over the noise. "I'm really, really sorry."

She tried to bolt, but Carter's hands caught her around the waist and spun her in a full circle, laughing. "Happy New Year, Hannah Mitchell!" He set her on her feet, steadying her. "That was absolutely brilliant!"

Hannah blinked, dizzy from both the spin and Carter's reaction. "What?"

"The way you tricked us! Luke and I never saw it coming."

"You're not mad?" she asked, searching Luke's face and then Carter's for any signs of hurt feelings.

"Mad?" Luke asked, his expression a mixture of amusement and admiration. "Are you kidding? That was the ultimate New Year's Eve prank."

Carter slung an arm around her shoulders and grinned at Luke. "I think we've corrupted her. All that competition brought out her wild side."

Hannah rolled her eyes. "I'm right here, Guys."

Luke leaned in and whispered in her ear. "I know you are. But maybe you shouldn't be. Maybe you should be looking for that guy you kissed. He seemed a little rattled."

Hannah's stomach flipped. "You're right," she said. She whipped around, scanning the crowd for Ben's tall frame.

"Lose something?" Wyatt asked from behind the bar.

"A guy. Brown hair. Gray stetson. I wanted to

apologize for, uh, dragging him into the midnight kissing thing."

Wyatt grinned. "Dragging? More like knocked the poor man sideways! He didn't see it coming, I promise you that."

"Neither did we," Carter said.

Wyatt leaned against the bar. "Pretty sure he left right after that kiss. With LeAnne."

"Oh, no." Hannah's heart sank. "Did I just kiss LeAnne's date right in front of her? Did they leave because of me?" The thought made her queasy.

"Don't worry," Wyatt said, shaking his head. "LeAnne didn't seem upset. She was laughing when they left."

"I hope you're right. But still—I can't believe I did that. I kissed a stranger—a perfect stranger!"

"So what?" Luke said. "It's New Year's Eve. I'm pretty sure it's not the first time he's been kissed under the mistletoe at midnight."

"You didn't see his face," Hannah said, twisting a curl around her finger. "He looked... completely shocked."

"Well, of course he was shocked," Carter said. "It's not every day a beautiful woman picks you over the most handsome guy in the room—me!"

Luke rolled his eyes. "Not to mention the most modest."

Hannah barely heard their banter. Her mind was spinning, replaying those few seconds under the mistletoe. The way Ben's eyes had widened. The warmth of his hand on her waist. The feel of his lips against hers.

Carter waved his hand in front of her face, bringing her back to the present. "Hannah, your kiss didn't drive him away. If anything, it probably made his night."

"You think?"

"I don't think. I know," Carter said, with absolute certainty. "Trust me, a surprise kiss from a beautiful woman is never a bad thing."

"He's right," Luke said. "You're making this into a bigger deal than it is." He gave her shoulder a reassuring squeeze. "Now, let's go see what Mrs. K. just put out for a midnight snack. I'm starved."

Three

HANNAH

HANNAH PULLED her car into the church parking lot, ice and snow crunching beneath her tires. She'd parked here a thousand times before—for Sunday services, Bible study meetings, potlucks—but today felt different. She wasn't here just to talk about the Winter Festival. After two days of replaying that midnight kiss in her mind, she needed Pastor John's steady voice and calm good sense.

She sat in the car for a long moment, hands clamped around the wheel. Even with her eyes open, she could still feel Ben's lips on hers, warm and soft. The memory had haunted her through a never-ending New Year's Day with her family: her sisters giggling, her brothers raising eyebrows and asking pointed questions about the Rusty Spur, her parents ignoring the whole thing.

And if her family was bad, the newspaper office yesterday was worse. Alyssa had peppered her with questions about how she ended up kissing a complete stranger until Hannah had finally told her everything. Or almost everything. She'd left out one minor detail: how the kiss had rocked her to her core. How every time she closed her eyes, she saw Ben's stunned expression, felt his hand on her waist, a touch so warm and solid it had sent tingles all the way up her spine. How she hadn't been able to stop thinking about him since, wondering if and when she'd see him again.

Pastor John's office sat in the back of the church, past the fellowship hall—the same hall that would host the Winter Festival in February. Her folder was bursting with papers filled with notes and ideas. Silent auction, chili cook-off, carnival games for the kids. She may not have willingly volunteered for the position, but now that she was in charge, she was determined to make it their best festival ever.

She filled her bottle at the water fountain

and took a moment to breathe. Pastor John was her rock. He had been there for everything: Sunday School, high school shenanigans, the year her grandfather died.

And when the church council had asked her to chair the Winter Festival, Pastor John had promised to guide her through every step. If anyone could untangle her confused feelings about that midnight kiss, it was Pastor John.

Hannah rounded the corner and almost collided with Mrs. Peterson, the church secretary. The model of efficiency, today she wore a chunky cardigan, denim skirt, and had a pencil tucked behind her ear.

"There you are, Hannah! I thought maybe you'd decided to skip this meeting."

"Never," Hannah said, a little breathless. "Just running a few minutes late. Is Pastor John ready?"

Mrs. Peterson's eyebrows went way up. "Didn't you get my email? I sent it last week."

A ripple of unease ran through Hannah. "What email?"

"About Pastor John's knee surgery. The doctors bumped it up. He left for Omaha yesterday. He'll be out for three months, maybe longer."

"Three months?" Hannah's voice rose an octave. The folder nearly slipped from her hands. "But... the Winter Festival. We were supposed to finalize everything today. Pastor John promised he'd help me through it. I—I can't do this without him."

The panic must have shown on her face because Mrs. Peterson immediately reached out and patted her shoulder. "Now, now. Don't you fret. The church council's got it all handled. They've hired an interim pastor to fill in while Pastor John recovers."

She gave Hannah's shoulder another reassuring pat. "He knows all about the Festival, dear. Pastor John made sure of it. The new pastor is fully prepared to help you through every bit of it."

Hannah tried to steady her breathing. "He... he knows about the Festival?"

"Every detail. Pastor John spent hours with him yesterday, going over everything. You're in good hands, I promise."

Mrs. Peterson leaned in, lowering her voice. "He's young, but comes highly recommended.

Top of his class at seminary, I heard. I'm pretty sure you'll get along just fine."

Mrs. Peterson's wink was not lost on her. What on earth was that about? Hannah tried to picture herself "getting along" with a pastor her own age—a person who'd probably use Instagram to share Bible verses and wore sneakers and blue jeans to church.

Maybe Mrs. Peterson was trying to play matchmaker. That thought made her skin prickle. Why, oh why, did Pastor John have to have his surgery now, when she needed him so badly?

Hannah nodded, swallowing her lingering anxiety. At least this new pastor knew about the Festival. She wouldn't have to start completely from scratch. But there was no way she could talk to him about what happened on New Year's Eve. Pastor John knew her inside and out. This new guy wouldn't.

"I guess I'd better introduce myself," she said.

"He's in Pastor John's office. Well, it's his office for now, I suppose." Mrs. Peterson gave her an encouraging nod. "Go on in. He's expecting you."

Hannah thanked her and headed down the hall. She stopped outside the familiar oak door, her hand hovering over the wood for a beat before she knocked.

"Come in."

She squared her shoulders, mustered up her best "Welcome to Bluestem" speech, and pushed open the door.

But when she stepped inside, her greeting shriveled in her throat. There, hanging prominently on the coat rack, was a gray Stetson. And behind Pastor John's old desk, surrounded by boxes of books, was a tall, dark, and handsome man. A man she'd kissed—impulsively, without thinking it through—on New Year's Eve.

Mrs. Peterson's knowing wink suddenly made perfect sense.

She froze in the doorway, hand locked on the knob, mouth hanging open. Her festival folder slipped from her fingers; papers fluttered everywhere. Her pen rolled under Pastor John's desk. No, his desk now. Pastor Ben's desk.

"I—you—" Hannah dropped to her knees, scrambling to gather the papers, grateful for the excuse to duck her head and hide her burning cheeks.

"Here, let me help." Ben was beside her in an instant, kneeling to scoop up the papers with impossibly quick efficiency. Their shoulders nearly bumped in the scramble, and Hannah was suddenly aware of just how small this office was.

She couldn't look at him. Couldn't breathe. Couldn't think. The memory of that impulsive kiss burned in her mind, searing away all coherent thought. She'd kissed the pastor. On the mouth. In a bar.

She was going straight to hell.

"I think that's all of them," Ben said, handing over a tidy stack. His fingers brushed against hers, and Hannah jerked back as if touched by a live wire.

"Thank you," she managed, her voice a strangled whisper. She clutched the papers to her chest like a shield.

Ben stood and offered his hand to help her up. Hannah stared at it for a long moment before accepting. His palm was warm and solid against hers, and the casual touch sent another wave of electricity through her.

She tried to swallow, but her throat was too tight. "You're... the interim pastor?" Her voice cracked on the words.

"I am," he said, holding her gaze with a small, lopsided smile. His voice was steady, like nothing unusual had ever happened between them.

Hannah's gaze darted around the office, desperate for something to look at besides Ben's face. Pastor John's familiar space was already transforming. The photo of Pastor John's wife was gone from the desk, replaced by a stack of theology books. A small plant she didn't recognize sat by the window, and Ben's jacket hung over the back of Pastor John's chair like it belonged there.

Even the air smelled different—less lemon polish and peppermints, more coffee and cologne. That same leather-and-spice scent that had gotten her into trouble on New Year's Eve.

Ben shoved a couple of boxes out of the way and gestured toward the chair across from his desk. "Please, sit down. I'm glad you could make it this morning."

Hannah sank into the chair, clinging to her folder like a life preserver. "Yes," she said, the word coming out as barely more than a whisper. She cleared her throat and tried again. "Thank you for agreeing to meet with me about the Festival."

Ben settled in across from her, leaning his elbows on the desk. "LeAnne's been singing its praises since I got here. She said the whole town looks forward to it."

Hannah nodded stiffly, her mind racing for something safe to talk about. Anything to fill the awkward silence stretching between them. "How... how do you like the Whitemore Hotel?" The words tumbled out in a rush. "LeAnne runs a wonderful place. The rooms are so charming, and her breakfasts are legendary."

"It's perfect," Ben said. "Much nicer than a chain hotel. LeAnne's been incredibly welcoming."

The way he said LeAnne's name—warm, familiar—made something twist in Hannah's stomach. LeAnne had introduced Ben as her guest. And Wyatt said she hadn't looked upset when they left. But had they actually been on a date that night?

It made sense. LeAnne was beautiful and single and ran the most romantic bed-and-breakfast in three counties. Hannah tried to remember the scene at their table: LeAnne in that gorgeous green velvet dress, her hands fluttering as she talked, Ben listening with that attentive smile.

Hannah's cheeks burned hotter. That would explain why they'd left so quickly after midnight —Ben mortified by her impulsive kiss, LeAnne hurt and confused, just pretending to act like it was funny.

"So," she said, her voice still wobbly, "you've been a minister for…?"

"Five years," he said. "I was an associate pastor in Lincoln before this. When the district superintendent called about this interim job, it seemed like a good fit. I've always wanted to live in a small town."

She nodded, pretending this was just a normal conversation, like she hadn't ambushed him under the mistletoe just three nights ago.

"The Festival committee will be excited to meet you," she said. "We have our first meeting next week, but I can catch you up on what we've planned so far."

"That would be great. Pastor John said you've worked at the Festival for years."

"Since I was old enough to sell raffle tickets." She flipped open her folder and started talking about the plans for this year's festival. For the next twenty minutes, they went over everything —silent auction items, volunteer sign-ups, the bake sale. Ben listened to every word, asked good questions, and even tossed out a few ideas of his own. As they talked, Hannah began to relax. She could do this. Of course she could.

But every time her gaze landed on his crisp white clerical collar, it all came rushing back. She'd kissed the new pastor. In a bar. In front of half the town.

"I think we've got a good start here," Ben said finally, closing his notebook. "Thanks for coming in today and going over this with me."

Hannah nodded and gathered her things together. "You're welcome. Now I'll get out of your way so you can finish unpacking." She gestured to the boxes still stacked against the wall.

"Before you go..." Ben's voice softened, gentler now. "I think we should *probably* talk about what happened on New Year's Eve."

Four

BEN WATCHED Hannah freeze at his words, the color draining from her face. He'd known this moment was coming as soon as Mrs. Peterson had mentioned their meeting. He'd spent most of the morning bracing himself, sifting through scenarios, trying to gauge the best way to handle it.

For the past two days, he'd replayed the party in his mind, frame by frame: Hannah's cheeks turning a delicate pink when LeAnne introduced them; the way her silver dress caught the light as she danced with Carter and Luke; the vulnerability in her green eyes as she'd glanced at the mistletoe hanging above their heads.

He'd planned to leave well before midnight,

but found himself lingering, watching the three of them, unable to tear himself away. They'd been so carefree, so comfortable with each other, and he'd found himself envious of their easy camaraderie.

He'd never been good at that kind of spontaneous fun.

And when she'd kissed him, he'd felt something stir in his chest—something he hadn't felt in a long time.

Now here she was, clutching that folder of hers like it was a life preserver, her eyes wide with mortification.

"I really need to get going," Hannah said, backing toward the door. "I work at the Gazette and—"

"Hannah." Ben fought to keep his voice steady. "Please. Sit down."

She collapsed into the chair as if her legs had given out. Ben tried to project an air of calm he didn't entirely feel. This was delicate territory. He'd dealt with plenty of awkward pastoral situations during his years of ministry, but none quite like this.

"I'm so sorry," Hannah whispered, staring at her lap. "It was just... Luke and Carter were having this dumb competition about who would get a midnight kiss, and I wanted to surprise them, and you were there, and—"

Ben opened his mouth to interrupt, but she barreled forward.

"It was impulsive, which is… honestly, if you ask anyone in town, they'll say that's my thing. Acting before I think. But I don't usually kiss people I've just met, especially not ones who are on a date—"

"Hannah." Ben tried again, but she kept going, words tumbling out faster now.

"I was going to talk to Pastor John about it today. Pastor John always helps me figure out why I do the things I do. Like why I promised to kiss someone under the mistletoe at midnight anyway. And why I kissed you, instead of Carter or Luke."

Ben felt a smile tugging at his lips despite himself. There was something endearing about her rambling confession, the way she was trying so hard to explain. He'd already pieced together most of it—that she'd had no idea who he was, that the kiss had been part of some friendly competition, that she was absolutely mortified now.

"Hannah, stop!" he said, letting a hint of laughter into his voice.

She finally looked up at him, her eyes wide and uncertain.

Time to put her out of her misery. "It's all right. Really. First off—LeAnne and I weren't on a date."

Relief flickered across her face. "You weren't?"

"No. LeAnne thought the party would be a nice way for me to meet a few people from the community before officially starting work." He paused, choosing his words carefully. "And second, you have nothing to apologize for. It was midnight, it was New Year's Eve, and we shared a kiss."

"But I basically tackled you. In public. And now you're my pastor and..." Her voice cracked. "I kissed my pastor."

Ben couldn't help the smile that spread across his face. "Technically, I wasn't your pastor yet."

She blinked at him. "It's not funny."

"I know." He sobered, leaning forward. He needed her to understand that he wasn't making light of her distress. "I'm just trying to say that what happened was completely innocent. We were two strangers who shared a traditional New Year's Eve kiss under the mistletoe."

And it had been innocent. Sweet, even. The kind of moment that, under different circumstances, might have led to coffee the next day, a phone number exchanged, the beginning of something.

But these weren't different circumstances. He *was* her pastor now, and that changed everything.

Ben rested his arms on the desk, meeting her eyes directly. "Look, I know this is awkward. For both of us. But I'd like to move past this, if we could. Start again?"

He watched her take a deep breath, saw her shoulders relax slightly. "Okay," she said, nodding.

"Good." Ben stood and walked around the desk, extending his hand "I'm Pastor Ben Landry. Nice to meet you, Hannah Mitchell."

She slid her hand into his, and Ben felt that same spark of connection he'd felt on New Year's Eve. He ignored it, focusing instead on the professional distance he needed to maintain.

"Nice to meet you too, Pastor Ben," she said, and he caught the hint of a smile on her lips.

Before she left, Ben knew he needed to say one more thing. Pastor John had mentioned that Hannah often came to him for guidance, and Ben didn't want her to feel like she'd lost that resource.

"Hannah, I know you wanted to meet with Pastor John today. And I know I'm not him. But I've been told I'm a pretty good listener. If you ever want to talk, my door's always open."

"Thank you." She hesitated, then offered a crooked smile. "But I should warn you, I make a lot of impulsive decisions that need talking through."

Ben laughed. He liked her honesty, her self-awareness. "Impulsive decisions are my specialty."

"I really *do* need to get to work," Hannah said, getting to her feet. "But I'll email you the committee list and meeting schedule later today."

"I'd appreciate that." Ben walked her to the door, very aware of the physical distance he maintained between them. "And Hannah? I meant what I said. If you need to talk, about anything, I'm here."

For a moment, something flickered in her eyes—loneliness, maybe, or uncertainty—and Ben found himself wanting to know more. Wanting to understand what was behind that impulsive kiss, what had driven her to seek Pastor John's counsel today.

She shifted her weight from one foot to the other, clutching the folder tighter against her chest. The moment stretched between them, filled with things unsaid, possibilities neither of them could acknowledge.

Then she just gave him a quick smile. "Thanks. I'll keep that in mind," she said, and stepped into the hallway.

"I'll see you on Sunday," Ben said.

He watched her steps falter, saw her shoulders stiffen, and he knew what she was thinking. Sunday. His first sermon. The whole church watching, including everyone who'd witnessed that midnight kiss.

As Hannah turned the corner, he sighed and closed the door. He straightened a pile of books on his desk, his fingers lingering on the leather-bound Bible his grandfather had given him when he started seminary.

He sank into the chair, running a hand through his hair. The meeting with Hannah had gone... better than he'd expected. So why did he feel this strange sense of disappointment?

He shook his head, pulling his sermon notes toward him. He knew why. Because Hannah Mitchell was exactly the kind of woman who would've caught his attention under normal circumstances. Warm, genuine, unafraid to be herself. The kind of woman who kissed strangers at midnight and then showed up to apologize with her heart on her sleeve.

But these weren't normal circumstances. He was her pastor. She was his parishioner. Ben had watched colleagues cross those lines and seen the devastation that followed—broken congregations, shattered trust, ruined lives.

He was only here for a short time. An interim pastor—in search of a congregation of his own. He wouldn't make that mistake. Couldn't make that mistake.

No, better to keep things professional. Friendly, but with boundaries firmly in place. He could be her pastor, offering guidance and support when she needed it. That would have to be enough.

And if a small part of him wished things could be different—well, he'd learned to live with disappointment before. He could do it again.

The important thing was doing right by his calling, by this congregation, and by Hannah herself. Even if it meant ignoring the ache in his chest every time he thought about that midnight kiss under the mistletoe.

Five

HANNAH PUSHED OPEN the door to the Bluestem Gazette, her curly red hair slightly disheveled from the January wind and her cheeks flushed from the cold. Or maybe from embarrassment. She couldn't tell anymore.

She ducked inside, glad to find the front office empty for once. No Lenny hunched over the typesetting machine in the back. No Maggie, going over her editorial page with him. No Alyssa, conferring with one or both of them about her next story. If Hannah was lucky, she would not have to talk to anyone for the rest of the day.

She shrugged out of her coat, hung it on a wooden peg by the door, then tip-toed to her desk. She set her folder down, booted up her computer, and tried to settle into her routine. But her mind kept circling back to that meeting with Ben. Pastor Ben, she reminded herself, wincing at the image of his clerical collar.

She groaned under her breath and rifled through a stack of papers, not really seeing them. Subscription renewals, classified ads, a handful of sticky notes in Maggie's looping script. But all she could hear was Ben's voice: "Technically, I wasn't your pastor yet."

"You're back early." Alyssa poked her head out of her office, making Hannah jump. "How did the meeting go with Pastor John?"

Hannah kept her gaze locked on the paperwork in front of her. "It, um... it didn't. Pastor John's in Omaha for knee surgery." She heard the quiver in her voice, but kept going. "So the church council hired someone to fill in for him. An interim pastor."

Alyssa waited. When Hannah didn't say anything more, she prompted, "And? How was he? Nice? Scary? Ancient?"

Hannah picked up a pen and began clicking it open and closed, over and over again. "I don't want to talk about it right now," she said, her voice flat. "It's just... I have a lot of work to do."

Alyssa reached out and took the pen from Hannah's hand. "Hannah. What happened? I've never seen you this flustered."

Hannah finally found the courage to look Alyssa in the face. "Nothing much. Really. But I think I want to resign as chair of the Winter Festival."

"What?" Alyssa's eyes went wide. "Why? You've been working on those plans for the past two months."

"I know, but..." Hannah stopped herself. She couldn't explain, not without telling Alyssa everything, and she wasn't ready for that conversation. Not here. Not now. Not even with herself.

Because if she was honest, it wasn't the gossip that worried her, or even the embarrassment of having kissed a stranger that turned out to be the pastor. It was the fact that she'd felt something during that stupid kiss. That she'd spent the last two days replaying it, over and over. Wondering when she'd see Ben again, what he'd say, what she'd say. The one thing she never expected him to say was that he was the new pastor at their church.

Alyssa studied her for a short time, then stood up. "Don't go anywhere. I'll be right back." She turned and headed straight for Maggie's office.

Hannah watched as Alyssa knocked on their boss's door, then slipped inside. When Alyssa reappeared, she marched to the front door and grabbed both their coats from the coat rack.

"Come on," she said, holding out Hannah's coat. "We're going to lunch."

Hannah stared at her in surprise. "Now? But I just got here. I have a mountain of subscriptions to process and I'm behind on the ad proofs and—"

"They'll wait." Alyssa jiggled the coat. "We're going to the Rusty Spur."

"The Rusty Spur? On a Tuesday? It's barely eleven-thirty."

"Exactly. We'll beat the rush." Alyssa's tone softened, but her eyes remained firm. "We're going to lunch, and you're going to tell me everything." She raised her hand, silencing any protest. "Don't even try to argue."

Hannah looked at Alyssa, then at the pile of

work on her desk, and finally at the folder containing all her Festival plans. "You're not going to let this go, are you?"

"Not a chance. Now, come on. Let's go sabotage our New Year's resolutions with Wyatt's chili and a couple of Mrs. K's oversized cinnamon rolls."

Hannah stood, accepting the coat with a sigh.

"That's my girl," Alyssa said, giving her an encouraging nod. "And don't worry. Whatever it is, it can't possibly be as bad as you think."

Hannah slipped her arms into her coat sleeves and managed a weak laugh. "Trust me," she said. "It's worse. Much, much worse!"

The Rusty Spur was already half full. Hannah paused and scanned for a booth where she and Alyssa could talk without half the town listening in.

"Hannah! Lyss! Over here!"

Hannah froze at the sound of Riley Manchester's voice. There, at a table by the window, sat Riley, Carter, and Luke, the last three people she wanted to see right now. Well, except for maybe Ben.

"Great," she said. "Just perfect."

Alyssa squeezed her arm. "We don't have to join them. We can still grab a booth."

Hannah hesitated, glancing between the welcoming grins of the three men and the increasingly crowded dining area. She chewed her bottom lip, weighing her options. She could avoid them, hide in a corner booth, and just tell Alyssa. Or... she could get it over with and tell them all at once. By Sunday, the whole town would know, anyway.

"It's fine," she said, giving in to fate.

Alyssa eyed her. "You sure?"

Hannah nodded, hoping she looked more confident than she felt.

By the time they reached the table, Riley had already flagged down Mrs. K. for extra menus and a fresh pot of coffee. "Well, well, look who's finally taking a lunch break," he said, scooting over to make room.

Alyssa slid in beside him. Hannah settled in between Carter and Luke.

Mrs. K. appeared, notepad in hand. "If it isn't two of my favorite girls. Did you come for Wyatt's chili special? Or is it just the company?" She gave Riley a wink before pouring coffee for everyone.

"Wyatt's chili special and the company!" Alyssa said, smiling.

"I'll get that order in for you right now," Mrs. K. said, and vanished back to the kitchen.

"What brings you two here in the middle of a workday?" Luke asked. "Shouldn't you be at the Gazette, making sure the good people of Bluestem know what's happening with the School Board's budget?"

Hannah shot Alyssa a pleading look. Her friend had dragged her here; the least she could do was get the conversation started.

Alyssa gave a tiny nod of understanding. "Hannah had a meeting this morning at the church, to talk about the Winter Festival. When she got back, she was pretty upset, so I suggested we take a break and talk about it."

Riley's eyes went wide. "Don't tell me you set off the fire alarm again."

"No, I did not," Hannah said, trying not to sound annoyed. "And anyway, we all know the altar candles are way too close to the smoke detector."

Carter laughed. "I'll never forget the look on Pastor John's face when the whole volunteer fire department rolled up outside the church."

"It's not about candles or alarms," Hannah said. "But it is about Pastor John." Her fingers trembled slightly, and she tucked them into her lap. "He's in Omaha, having knee surgery."

"Oh, no!" Luke said. "Will he be back in time for the Festival?"

"Mrs. Peterson said he probably won't be back for three months." Hannah picked up her napkin and started folding it into neat little squares, focusing on the edges and not on the four sets of eyes waiting for her to go on. "The church council hired someone to fill in while he's gone. An interim pastor."

Riley took a sip of his water. "Anyone we know?"

Hannah's cheeks burned. "No. Yes. Sort of." She smoothed her napkin flat, then folded it again. "His name is Ben Landry."

Alyssa's jaw dropped. "Ben? As in Mistletoe Ben? New Year's Eve Ben? *That* Ben?"

"The guy you kissed instead of *me*?" Carter asked.

"Or *me*?" Luke added.

Hannah squeezed her eyes shut and wished she could disappear. "Yes. *That* Ben."

Six

HANNAH

THE TABLE WENT SILENT. Hannah felt the weight of four stares but refused to look up, focusing instead on the napkin she was strangling in her lap.

A muffled snort broke the silence. Hannah's head jerked up to find Carter with his fist pressed against his mouth, shoulders quivering. She glanced at Luke, who'd pressed his lips into a thin line while the corners of his eyes crinkled. Even Riley—after a brief, valiant attempt at a sympathetic expression—surrendered to the moment. Within seconds, all three men were howling with laughter, drawing curious looks from neighboring tables.

"It's not funny," Hannah hissed, her cheeks

burning as more and more diners looked their way. "Will you please stop?"

That only made them laugh harder. Carter was wheezing now, and Luke had to dab at his eyes with a corner of his napkin.

"Fine, laugh all you want," Hannah said. She folded her arms tightly across her chest. "But you wouldn't be laughing if you'd been there this morning."

Luke gulped a breath, trying to recover. "I'm sorry, Hannah, but you have to admit—it's kind of funny."

"Kind of?" Carter said, still wiping away tears. "It's the funniest thing I've heard all year."

Hannah glared at him. "The year is three days old."

"Still counts," Carter said.

Alyssa reached across the table and gently pried the napkin from Hannah's fist. "Hannah, it's not that big of a deal. It was just a kiss." But her lips twitched, and she stared down at her glass of water.

Hannah yanked her hand back. "A little support would be nice."

"I'm sorry," Alyssa said, pressing her fingertips to her mouth. "I really am trying."

"It's easy for you all to laugh," Hannah said. The heat was crawling up her neck now. "You didn't see Mrs. Peterson. She winked at me before she sent me back to his office. Said she was sure I'd get along with the 'new pastor' just fine." Hannah's voice rose slightly, and she caught a movement in her peripheral vision. Two men at the bar—Darryl Hoffman and his brother Stan—were staring at her. "And look! People are already talking about it."

"I'm sure they're not—"

"They are!" Hannah said. "Darryl just pointed at me. I saw him."

"So what's your plan?" Luke asked. "Go into hiding until the man leaves town?"

Hannah nodded, completely serious. "That's exactly what I'm going to do. I'll resign as chair of the Winter Festival and find a replacement. Maybe I'll tell everyone I have mono. That should keep me home for a month, at least."

"Makes perfect sense to me," Riley said. "Mono is the kissing disease, after all."

The three guys burst out laughing again, while Alyssa's jaw dropped. "Riley Manchester, I cannot believe you just said that."

"What? It's true!" Riley said, shrugging. "If

you're going to fake an illness, might as well pick one that fits the crime."

Hannah groaned and buried her face in her hands.

Mrs. K. appeared at their table, balancing a tray filled with steaming bowls of chili and a plate of enormous cinnamon rolls still warm from the oven. "Here we go!" she said, setting everything down. "I added a few extra rolls for the guys."

She surveyed the table, taking in the red faces and shaking shoulders. "Do I even want to know what's so funny?"

"No, you don't," Hannah said. "Trust me."

"Well, whatever it is, these rolls will fix it right up." Mrs. K. studied her for a moment longer, then patted her shoulder. "Now, eat your lunch before it gets cold."

Hannah managed a weak smile. "Thank you, Mrs. K."

Mrs. K. headed back to the kitchen, refilling water glasses as she went.

Hannah stared at her chili. She wasn't hungry anymore. "As soon as we get back to the Gazette, I'm calling Mrs. Peterson. I'll ask her to let Pastor Ben know I'm resigning."

"Hannah, that's ridiculous." Alyssa shook her head. "You've been working on this festival for months. You can't quit over one awkward moment."

"Awkward moment?" Hannah's voice rose to a squeak. "I kissed the new pastor! With half the town watching!" She stirred her chili, trying to keep her hands from shaking. "Maybe I'll just move. I've always wanted to live in California."

"Now you're just being dramatic," Luke said, tearing a cinnamon roll in half.

"I'm not being dramatic," Hannah said, even as she recognized the note of hysteria creeping into her voice. "I'm just being practical."

"Well, practically speaking, that's the worst idea I've ever heard," he said.

"How is it the worst?" Hannah put her spoon down and glared at him. "California has beaches. Sunshine. And nobody knows I kissed our pastor."

"Come on, Hannah. You'd be miserable there," Alyssa said. "And I'd be miserable here, without you."

Hannah nodded. "I know. I just don't know what else to do. This is a nightmare. An absolute nightmare."

"Maybe not." Riley's voice cut through Hannah's spiral of self-pity like a knife through butter. He looked at Luke and Carter, a sly grin curling his lips. "I've got a way to make everyone forget all about what you did on New Year's Eve."

That got Hannah's attention. She straightened a bit in her seat, a few wild red curls falling into her eyes. "How?" She was desperate enough to try any solution, no matter how absurd.

Riley grinned. "If you want the town to forget about that kiss, you just have to give them something new to talk about."

"Like what?" Hannah asked, not sure she liked where this was going.

He barely paused. "Like who Hannah Mitchell is going to be kissing on Valentine's Day!"

Her jaw dropped. "No." It came out louder than she intended; heads turned at the next table. She lowered her voice. "Absolutely not. My kissing days are over. Done." She slashed her hand in front of her. "My lips are officially in retirement."

Luke just laughed, shaking his head as he broke off another chunk of cinnamon roll. "You can't retire your lips at thirty, Hannah Banana. Besides, Riley's got a point. You still owe Carter or me a kiss. Valentine's Day works just as well as New Year's Eve."

"I agree," Carter said, nodding. "And as far as Pastor Ben knows, Luke and I are both crazy about you. So the whole thing is totally believable."

Hannah frowned. "What?"

"Think about it," Carter said. "The three of us were together all night on New Year's Eve. Luke and I were dancing with you, bringing you drinks, acting like total fools."

Alyssa's lips curved into a smile. "I hate to admit it, but the guys are actually making sense. From Ben's viewpoint, it probably looked like you had two men competing to be your boyfriend that entire night."

Hannah twisted a curl around her finger, remembering. "He did say something like that, right before . . . well, you know." A reluctant smile tugged at her lips. "He asked if I was taking a break from my 'fan club.'"

Carter's face lit up. "Perfect. That's exactly what we'll be." He straightened in his chair and cleared his throat dramatically. "This meeting of the Hannah Mitchell Fan Club is now in session. First order of business . . ." He tapped his spoon against his water glass like a gavel. "Never allow Hannah to be alone with Pastor Ben."

Hannah rolled her eyes, but couldn't help smiling just a little. "Don't be ridiculous, Carter. I don't need a bodyguard. He's a pastor."

Carter shook his head, eyes solemn. "It's not for your protection. It's for his. We can't have you attacking the poor man every time you see him."

"I did not attack him!" Hannah punched Carter in the arm, hard enough to make him yelp.

"Ow! That hurt!" Carter rubbed his upper arm, but his grin remained firmly in place.

Everyone laughed, including Hannah, and she felt the knot in her chest loosen, just a little.

"All joking aside," Riley said, once their laughter faded, "having these two knuckleheads openly compete for your attention will be the perfect distraction. By February, no one will even be thinking about that New Year's Eve kiss."

Hannah chewed on a cinnamon roll, considering the idea. She looked at Luke. "What about that nurse you're seeing in Valentine? Won't she have something to say about you pretending to date me?"

Luke shrugged, his expression unconcerned. "If she can't understand that I'm just helping a friend out of a jam, then she's not the girl for me." He popped another piece of cinnamon roll into his mouth.

"Hey, what about me?" Carter asked. "Aren't you worried about *my* girlfriends?"

Hannah rolled her eyes. "All ten of them, you mean?"

"What can I say. I like to date," Carter said.

"Dating isn't the same as having a girl-friend," Riley said, smiling at Alyssa.

"Maybe I don't want to be tied down to one woman," Carter said, lifting his chin. "Maybe I'm just waiting for the right one to come along."

Hannah reached over and squeezed Carter's hand, her eyes meeting his. A familiar shadow passed across his face—one she'd seen countless times over the past fifteen years. They all knew exactly who he was waiting for.

Dani Hudson had left town right after breaking their engagement, taking a piece of Carter's heart with her. Everyone else in town might think Carter was playing the field, but his friends knew better. He was just marking time until Dani came home.

"Maybe the right one will come back, soon," she said.

Carter's smile turned wistful. "Maybe." He squeezed her hand back.

"So, it's decided," Riley said. "From now until Valentine's Day, Carter and Luke will compete for Hannah's affection, and the whole town will have something new to talk about."

Hannah opened her mouth to protest, then closed it again. Maybe this crazy scheme wasn't *such* a bad idea. If it would distract people from her mortifying moment with Pastor Ben, it *might* be worth a try. "Okay, so how would it actually work? You two just pretend to . . . what, exactly?"

"To date you, to see who you will choose to be your official boyfriend by Valentine's Day," Luke said. "And it's not pretend. I'm deadly serious about this! I will be the sole owner of those lips of yours by Valentine's Day!" He put both of his hands over his own heart and sighed dramatically.

Carter scoffed. "Please. You wouldn't know what to do with her lips if she gift-wrapped them for you."

"See?" Riley gestured between the two men. "The competition is already fierce."

Hannah shook her head, fighting a smile. "This is ridiculous."

"Just ridiculous enough to work," Alyssa said. "Two eligible bachelors fighting over the town's most eligible bachelorette? It's like a reality TV show, right here in Bluestem."

"And what happens on Valentine's Day? When I'm supposed to kiss one of these guys?" Hannah asked, still skeptical.

Riley shrugged. "By then, New Year's Eve will be old news. You can pick one of them, or neither of them. It doesn't matter. The point is to give the town something else to talk about between now and then."

Hannah sat back in her chair, her lunch forgotten. The plan was absurd. Childish, even. But, honestly? It was better than resigning as the chair of the Winter Festival committee, or hiding in her house, or moving to California.

"So, what do you say?" Carter asked, raising his glass. "Are you in?"

Hannah looked around the table at her friends: at Luke and Carter's mischievous and competitive grins, at Riley's practical confidence, at Alyssa's encouraging smile. She took a deep breath, let it out slowly, and lifted her glass in answer. "To the worst idea I've ever heard. Let's hope it actually works."

The five of them clinked glasses around the table, and Hannah felt the last of her panic melt away, replaced by an unexpected sense of relief. For the first time since she'd walked into Pastor John's office that morning and saw Ben, Hannah believed that maybe, just maybe, everything really would be okay.

Seven

BEN

BEN WOKE BEFORE HIS ALARM, the pale winter light just beginning to seep through the curtains of his room at the Whitemore Hotel. He lay still for a moment, listening to the old building creak and settle around him, feeling the weight of the day press against his chest.

His first sermon in Bluestem. His official introduction to the congregation that would be his flock for the next three months. He closed his eyes briefly, offering a silent prayer for guidance, before swinging his legs over the side of the bed.

The polished wooden floor was cold beneath his bare feet. Ben reached for his watch on the nightstand—5:47 a.m. Earlier than necessary, but sleep had been elusive, his mind too full of sermon notes and faces he'd yet to memorize. And one face in particular that he couldn't seem to forget.

Ben ran a hand through his hair and padded to the bathroom. This was not the time to be dwelling on a midnight kiss or the way Hannah's green eyes had widened in shock when she'd discovered who he was. Today was about his calling, his responsibility to the church who had welcomed him to Bluestem.

Twenty minutes later, freshly showered and shaved, Ben stood in the sitting room of his suite, staring at his reflection in the antique mirror. LeAnne had given him the William Jennings Bryan room. It was larger than he needed, with a separate bedroom and sitting area, but LeAnne had insisted it would give him space to work.

William Jennings Bryan was just a name from a history book to Ben—a politician known for his oratory. The kind of speaker who could hold thousands in the palm of his hand with nothing more than a few well-chosen words and an unwavering belief. Ben straightened his collar and wished some of that legendary eloquence would rub off on him today.

First-sermon jitters were nothing new. But this felt different. Pastor John was beloved in Bluestem—that much was clear from the way everyone spoke of him. Ben's task was to serve, to guide, to fill a temporary space without trying to replace the irreplaceable.

He moved to the desk where his sermon notes lay spread out, next to his Bible. "New beginnings," he murmured, scanning the pages. The theme had seemed perfect when he'd chosen it. A fresh start for a new year, for a congregation in transition, for a pastor taking on a temporary flock.

Now, with Hannah's startled face fresh in his mind, the words took on a different meaning.

Ben shook his head and reached for his navy suit jacket. He checked his reflection in the full-length mirror by the door. The man who looked back was everything a pastor should be: dignified, approachable, trustworthy.

He picked up his Bible and flipped it open to the passage he'd chosen for today's sermon. Isaiah 43:19. "See, I am doing a new thing! Now it springs up; do you not perceive it? I am making a way in the wilderness and streams in the wasteland."

New beginnings. Fresh starts.

He'd rehearsed this sermon a dozen times already, but he went through it again, pacing the small room as he spoke the words aloud. His voice was steady, confident. He hit each point with precision, building to the conclusion with practiced ease.

"God doesn't ask us to be perfect," he said to the empty room, "but to be willing. Willing to step forward into the unknown. Willing to trust that He's making a way, even when we can't see it yet."

The words felt hollow in his mouth. He stopped mid-stride and ran a hand over his face.

He was overthinking this. He knew he was overthinking this.

But every time he tried to focus, his mind wandered back to Hannah. To the way she'd looked in that silver dress, her red curls catching the light. To the conversation in his office, her obvious mortification, her stumbling apology. To the moment when he'd told her he hadn't been on a date with LeAnne, and something had shifted in her eyes—relief, maybe, or hope.

He shouldn't have noticed that. Shouldn't have cared.

Ben set down his pen and pressed his palms flat against the desk. The wood was cool and smooth under his hands, grounding him.

This was exactly why pastors needed boundaries. Why he'd always been so careful to maintain professional distance, especially with single women in his congregation. It wasn't about attraction—attraction was natural, human, inevitable. It was about protecting the integrity of his ministry, about ensuring that people could trust him without wondering about his motives.

And now, before he'd even preached his first sermon, those boundaries were already blurred.

At 7:30, Ben tucked his portfolio under his arm and headed downstairs. The scent of coffee and cinnamon greeted him, and he found LeAnne in the breakfast room, arranging a variety of pastries on a tiered stand.

"Ben! How are you feeling this morning?" she asked. "Nervous about your first sermon?"

"A little," he admitted, accepting the cup of coffee she poured for him. "It's always a challenge, stepping into someone else's pulpit."

LeAnne nodded, understanding in her eyes. She handed him a plate with a croissant and some fruit. "Here, you need something in your stomach before you face the congregation."

Ben accepted the plate, surprised at LeAnne's perception. "You always seem to know exactly what people need," he said, taking a bite of the warm pastry. The sweetness melted on his tongue, momentarily distracting him from his nerves. "It's truly a gift."

"Thank you. It's a trait I inherited from my mother. She taught me that hospitality is more than just a comfortable bed. It's about making people feel at home, especially when they're far from theirs."

Ben smiled at LeAnne's words, feeling a surge of gratitude for her kindness. "Well, you excel at it. I've never been so pampered."

"I'm glad to hear that." LeAnne refilled his coffee cup. "And don't worry about today. The congregation will love you. Just be yourself."

Be yourself. The advice followed Ben as he drove his Jeep through the quiet streets of Bluestem. But who exactly was that? The interim pastor who smiled, shook hands, and maintained appropriate professional boundaries; who'd come to Bluestem with a clear understanding of what his responsibilities were and what was expected of him?

Or the man who'd felt his pulse quicken when Hannah Mitchell had walked into his office, who'd looked into those green eyes and remembered, once again, that impulsive New Year's Eve kiss that melted his heart and had him dreaming of more.

And for the first time since he'd entered the seminary, he wasn't sure who he wanted to be more—the pastor or the man.

Eight

BEN

BEN PULLED his Jeep into the pastor's spot in the parking lot. He turned off the ignition and sat for a moment, studying the church that was his temporary spiritual home.

The morning sun glinted off the beautiful stained glass windows, each one a masterpiece of color and light. He gathered his Bible and portfolio, then stepped out into the crisp January air. His breath formed small clouds that dissipated into the clear blue sky. The cold nipped at his ears and nose as he made his way up the walkway, nodding to an older couple who approached from the opposite direction.

"Good morning," Ben said, his voice steady despite the fluttering in his stomach.

"Howdy, Pastor," the man said, tipping his hat. "I'm Lenny Beckett. This is my wife, Hattie. We're looking forward to your message today."

Ben smiled, appreciating the simple welcome. "Thanks. I hope it doesn't disappoint."

Inside, the church was warm and smelled of furniture polish and old wood. Ben checked his watch—thirty minutes until the service officially started—but the sanctuary already had a smattering of folks seated in the pews. He hung his coat on the rack in the entryway and straightened his collar.

Mrs. Peterson appeared at his elbow. "Good morning, Ben. How are you doing this morning?"

"I'm good," Ben said, forcing a smile that he hoped looked genuine. His throat felt tight. "Thank you for all your help this week. I really appreciate it."

She nodded. "Happy to be here for you, with whatever you need. The side room is open, if you'd like a moment before the service begins."

Ben nodded and slipped into the small preparation room just off the entryway. A narrow window offered a view of the parking lot, now filling with cars and trucks. Families walked toward the church, children bundled against the cold, their breath visible in the winter air.

He told himself he was simply observing the congregation, getting a feel for the community he'd be serving. That he wasn't waiting for any specific parishioner.

Except he was, and the lie gnawed at him.

He closed his eyes and pressed his forehead against the cool glass. "Lord, help me keep my focus where it needs to be," he prayed. "Help me serve these people well. Most importantly, help me remember why I'm here."

A soft knock interrupted his moment of quiet. Mrs. Peterson poked her head in. "Ten minutes, Ben."

The door clicked shut behind her, and Ben was alone again with his thoughts and his Bible. He opened it to Isaiah, running his finger along the familiar verse. The words had felt right when he'd chosen them, but now they seemed to mock him. New beginnings. Fresh starts. God making a way in the wilderness.

What wilderness had he wandered into?

The sanctuary was nearly full. Ben walked down the center aisle, nodding to the faces that turned toward him. Rows of wooden pews stretched before him, populated with faces both curious and welcoming. Some smiled encouragingly. Others studied him with the frank appraisal of people sizing up a stranger who would occupy their pulpit for the next three months. Children squirmed in their seats while parents shushed them with gentle hands.

But one face was conspicuously absent. Hannah was nowhere to be seen.

He reached the pulpit and set his Bible down, arranging his notes with careful precision. His hands were steadier than he'd expected, though his heart beat faster than usual. The organist transitioned into the opening hymn, and the congregation rose as one, hymnals opening, voices lifting.

Ben sang along, his baritone blending with the others, and felt some of his tension ease. This was familiar ground—worship, community, the shared rhythm of liturgy that had sustained believers for centuries. When the hymn ended and people settled back into their seats, he stepped up to the pulpit and adjusted his collar, a nervous habit he'd never quite broken.

"Good morning," he said, his voice catching slightly. He cleared his throat. "I'm Pastor Ben

Landry, and it's my privilege to be with you while Pastor John recovers."

A murmur of welcome rippled through the congregation. Ben smiled, feeling some of his tension ease. "Before I begin, I want to thank you all for your warm welcome to Bluestem. I've only been here a few days, but I already feel at home."

There were a few nods, and lots of smiles. Ben glanced down at his notes, then set them aside.

"Today I want to talk to you about new beginnings." He opened his Bible, though he didn't need to. The words were etched in his memory. "See, I am doing a new thing! Now it springs up; do you not perceive it? I am making a way in the wilderness and streams in the wasteland."

He looked up from the Bible, scanning the congregation. "The prophet Isaiah was speaking to the Israelites during their exile in Babylonia. They were far from home, feeling abandoned, wondering if God had forgotten them. And into that darkness, God spoke a word of hope. Not a promise that everything would go back to the way it was, but something different. Something new."

As he spoke, Ben found his rhythm, the nervousness fading as he focused on the message rather than himself. He moved away from the pulpit, hands gesturing to emphasize his points, voice rising and falling with the cadence of his thoughts.

"New beginnings aren't always easy, are they? Sometimes they're downright uncomfortable." A few knowing smiles appeared in the pews. "Sometimes they involve stepping into unfamiliar territory, meeting new people, forming new relationships."

He thought of Hannah then, of the shock in her green eyes when she realized who he was. Of the way she'd fled his office, her cheeks flushed with embarrassment. He scanned the pews once more.

"But here's what I have come to believe." His voice warmed with conviction. "God doesn't just help us endure change. He works through it. He uses transitions to show us new aspects of His character, to build our faith in unexpected ways, to create streams in the wasteland."

He paused, letting the words settle. A baby fussed somewhere in the back, then quieted.

"We're all in transition right now," Ben said.

"You're adjusting to a new pastor. I'm learning a new congregation. Pastor John is facing his own new beginning with his recovery. But in the midst of all this change, God is doing a new thing—making a way through whatever wilderness we're facing."

He glanced at a young family in the back pew, saw the mother's tired eyes, the father's protective arm around his children. He thought of the farmers and ranchers he'd met in town, facing another uncertain season. He thought of Mrs. Peterson, faithfully keeping the church running through an unexpected pastoral transition. He thought—though he tried not to—of Hannah, and the complicated new beginning thrust upon both of them.

"God doesn't ask us to be perfect," Ben said, returning to the pulpit. "He asks us to be willing. Willing to step forward into the unknown. Willing to trust that He's making a way, even when we can't see it yet. Willing to believe that new beginnings, however uncomfortable, are often exactly what we need."

He let the words hang in the air for a moment, then returned to his notes for the conclusion. His hands no longer trembled. His voice no longer wavered. This was what he'd been called to do—to speak truth, to offer hope, to point people toward something bigger than their own circumstances.

"So as we begin this new year together," Ben said, "I invite you to ask yourself: where is God doing a new thing in your life? Where is He making a way in your wilderness? And are you willing to trust Him enough to follow?"

He closed his Bible, a sense of peace settling over him. "Let us pray."

The congregation bowed their heads, and Ben spoke a blessing over them, his words simple and heartfelt. When he finished, the organist began the closing hymn, and people rose once more, voices lifting in song.

As the last notes faded and people began gathering their coats and Bibles, Ben stepped down from the pulpit. He'd made it through his first sermon. The congregation had been receptive, engaged, and welcoming.

But as people began filing out of the sanctuary toward the fellowship hall for morning coffee, Ben's gaze swept the room one more time, searching for a face he knew wouldn't be there. Hannah's absence spoke louder than any greeting could have.

For the next three months, this was his flock, his responsibility. All of them, including one red-haired woman who'd surprised them both with a New Year's kiss. Whatever awkwardness lay between them, Ben was determined to find a way forward. For the good of the congregation and for Hannah. For the sake of the Winter Festival. And perhaps, though he was reluctant to admit it even to himself, for the sake of his own peace of mind.

Nine

HANNAH

Hannah arrived at work Monday morning tired and groggy, the guilt from skipping church the day before still nagging her. She seldom missed a Sunday service, and never because she didn't want to go.

But yesterday morning, she'd stared at her ceiling and just ...didn't go to church. She couldn't face sitting in that pew while Ben stood at the pulpit, couldn't bear the sideways glances from everyone who'd witnessed that New Year's Eve kiss and recognized Ben as the man she'd ambushed at midnight. So she'd pulled the covers over her head and stayed there until noon, ignoring her mother's concerned texts and the hollow feeling in her chest.

She grimaced, pushed open the front door of the Gazette, and stepped inside. She set her coffee down, slipped off her coat, and then froze.

On her desk was a bouquet of flowers that definitely hadn't been there when she'd left on Friday. A rainbow crammed into a Mason jar, right next to her computer monitor.

She approached slowly, as if the flowers might be an illusion that would vanish if she moved too quickly. Winter in Nebraska meant bleak landscapes and brown grass; fresh flowers did not grow on every corner. Or on any corner, for that matter. Yet here they were: cheerful yellow sunflowers, white daisies, some blue flax, with sprigs of green nestled in between them all.

A small cream-colored card leaned against the jar. Hannah recognized Carter's bold handwriting immediately:

> *Hannah,*
> *Want to join me for a picnic lunch?*
> *I'll be at the Gazette at noon. Dress warm.*
> *Carter*

SHE TRACED a finger over the words, a smile tugging at her lips despite herself. Last week, she'd been on the verge of moving to California. Now, Carter Manchester was bringing her wildflowers and planning picnics. In January.

Hannah snapped a quick picture of the bouquet and texted it to Alyssa.

> Did you know about these?

The response was immediate.

> Maybe. How do you think they found their way to your desk?

Hannah grinned, then set to work. But she'd barely started on a stack of subscription renewals when her phone vibrated.

LUKE

> Good morning, Hannah. I know you have a busy day, between work and Carter. But please save tomorrow night for me!

Hannah smiled and texted a quick response.

> Tomorrow night is all yours.

She had just set her phone down when the front door opened, letting in a blast of cold air along with Lenny Beckett, the Gazette's typesetter. He stomped his boots on the welcome mat, his salt and pepper gray hair tousled from the wind, his eyes completely hidden behind wire-rimmed glasses fogged white from the sudden change of temperature.

Lenny pulled off his glasses and wiped them on his shirt. "Morning, Hannah. Missed you at church yesterday." As he slid the frames back onto his nose, his gaze landed on the jar of flowers, and his bushy eyebrows shot up. "Well, well. Flowers! What's the occasion?"

Hannah felt heat rise to her cheeks. "No special occasion. Just Carter Manchester, being thoughtful."

Lenny let out a low whistle. "Carter Manchester? He's a catch, that one. Richest rancher in five counties and as handsome as the day is long. Or so my wife tells me." He hung his coat on the rack and shuffled closer to inspect the bouquet.

Before Hannah could comment, her phone buzzed again. Another text from Luke.

I hear the best way to warm up on a chilly night is with a cozy dinner. I'll have my chariot at your house at six tomorrow night to pick you up!

Lenny peered over her shoulder at the phone, not even pretending to be subtle. "Flowers, and now dinner, too? That boy is going all out!"

Hannah flipped her phone face down on the paperwork. "That's not from Carter," she said, trying not to sound as flustered as she felt. "It's from Luke Merriwether."

Lenny's eyes narrowed. "The doc? Well, aren't you the popular one."

She shrugged. "It's... complicated."

"Complicated, eh?" Lenny barked out a laugh. "Two fellas chasing one gal. That's not just complicated. That's out-and-out trouble." He nodded toward the flowers. "Looks like the Manchester boy is winning, if you ask me. Flowers beat text messages any day."

"It's not a competition," Hannah said, then bit her lip, because that was exactly what it was supposed to look like.

"Sure it's not," Lenny said, his tone making it

clear he didn't believe her for a second. "That's why you're blushing redder than a sunburned farmhand in July." He shuffled off, shaking his head.

Hannah glanced from the wildflowers to Luke's messages. The plan was working. The gossip was already starting, right here in the Gazette office.

But as she touched the soft petals of a daisy, Ben's dimple flashed through her mind. If their scheme worked, everyone would soon forget about their New Year's Eve kiss. Everyone except her.

By mid-morning, Hannah's to-do list was a lost cause. She'd read the same invoice three times and still couldn't recall a single number. Her mind kept wandering to Carter's picnic plans and Luke's text messages. She had to admit; it felt good to be the center of attention, even if it was all for show.

At exactly 11:57, Carter's truck pulled up in front of the Gazette. And at 11:58, Luke's next text arrived.

> Flowers in January are a nice
> touch, but …

Hannah shook her head. Luke's competitive streak was showing. She typed:

> But what? Don't leave me hanging!

Three little dots appeared, then disappeared, then appeared again. Finally:

> But I guarantee tomorrow will be even better. Just wait and see.

She looked up, startled to find herself surrounded. Lenny had come back from his break early, declaring he wouldn't miss this for the world. Alyssa leaned against the door frame of her office, not even bothering to hide her phone, which she held up in front of her face, ready to take a photo. Even Maggie had taken this moment to step out of her office to refill her coffee.

Carter strode into the Gazette, picnic basket in one hand, portable heater in the other, blanket tucked under his arm. He wore a navy quilted vest over a crisp white shirt, which should have looked ridiculous with his mud-stained boots, but somehow didn't.

"You ready, Beautiful?" he asked, as if this was their everyday lunch routine.

She nodded her head, smiling. Only Carter could make a picnic in January seem romantic and fun.

Lenny pointed at the basket. "Picnicking in the dead of winter, Manchester? You trying to freeze the poor girl?"

Carter grinned. "Not to worry, Lenny. I came prepared. I'll keep our Hannah toasty warm, I promise."

"Smile, you two," Alyssa said as she snapped a picture.

"Make sure you get my good side," Carter said, winking at her.

Hannah bundled up, tucking her hands into thick wool mittens and winding her scarf around her neck. "Lead the way," she said, nodding toward the door. "And while we're eating lunch, you can tell me where you got flowers in January."

Carter's smile turned mysterious. "A gentleman never reveals his secrets. Let's just say I know people who know people."

Alyssa laughed. "In other words, you raided your sister Kate's greenhouse this morning."

Carter nodded. "Exactly."

They stepped outside into the crisp January air, the sky a perfect clear blue above them. They walked side by side down Main Street toward the town square, Hannah carrying the blanket. A handful of birds huddled under the war memorial, pecking half-heartedly at scattered popcorn, the only signs of life in the deserted square.

Carter led the way to the white gazebo in the center of the park. The snow had been cleared from the walkway, and twinkle lights wound around the railings, soft and golden in the late afternoon.

He spread the blanket over the bench, then stepped back with a flourish. "Your seat, Miss Mitchell."

Hannah stared at the bench as if it were poison. "Seriously, Carter. This is where you brought me for our first date? To the Hitching Bench? You know couples only sit here when they're about to get engaged."

He gave an exaggerated sigh. "The Hitching Bench? Is that what you call it? That sounds like a place you'd park a horse, not a heart. I prefer to think of it as the Bench of No Return."

"You're incorrigible," Hannah said, but she

couldn't help smiling as she settled onto the blanket-covered bench. The wood was still cold beneath her, but at least it was dry.

"And yet," he said, grinning, "here you are, voluntarily seated on Bluestem's most notorious piece of furniture."

Hannah rolled her eyes, but her smile lingered. The air was sharp, her breath white in the glow of the lights. For all his teasing, Carter had gone to a lot of trouble.

Carter set the portable heater at their feet and switched it on. Warm air immediately began circulating around their ankles. He poured cocoa from a thermos into two ceramic mugs, topping each with a dollop of whipped cream. "Careful. It's hot."

She took a sip and nearly burned her tongue. "Understatement of the year."

He shrugged, unpacking roast beef sandwiches, potato salad, and oatmeal cookies. "I would have made something fancier, but I sort of ran out of time."

A group of seniors power-walked past, slowing to stare. Carter waved and grinned. "Looks like our little picnic is getting some attention already."

Hannah groaned when she saw Mrs. Peterson in the group. She must have been on her lunch break from church.

She knew Mrs. Peterson wasn't a gossip, but would she say something to Ben about seeing them? And what if she did? Wasn't that part of the plan?

"You okay?" Carter asked, offering her a sandwich. "You got quiet all of a sudden."

"I'm fine. Just hungry." She took the sandwich and forced herself to forget about Mrs. Peterson. "Tell me something I don't know about the Manchesters."

Carter leaned back against one of the gazebo posts. "Did I ever told you about the time Riley and I let all the horses out of the corral?"

Hannah shook her head and bit into her sandwich. It was perfect—tender roast beef, just the right amount of mayo.

"We were little. About eleven and seven. I think. Dad had just gotten this new little filly from some hot shot horse trainer in Colorado. Riley bet me five dollars I couldn't ride her."

Carter took a drink of his hot chocolate. "Now, I knew better than to mess with Dad's horses, but five dollars was a fortune. And you know I can't back down from a challenge. Riley and I sneaked into the corral and I was just about to hook the gate when Kate came running and screaming, saying she was going to tell Dad. Spooked all of the horses good." Carter shook his head, grinning. "They took off in a dozen different directions, and Dad and I spent the rest of the night chasing after them."

"Oh, no!"

"Yep. Plus, Dad put me in charge of mucking out stalls for the next month. And Riley never did pay me that five dollars."

Hannah laughed, picturing the Manchester siblings as children, getting into mischief around the ranch. Carter had a way of telling stories that made her feel like she was right there with him, seeing everything through his eyes.

They swapped stories for nearly an hour, laughter echoing in the empty square. After they finished eating, Carter packed up the leftovers, shut down the heater, and walked her back to the Gazette.

"Thanks for having lunch with me."

"Thanks for asking," she said. "I had a really great time."

"Me, too," he said. "Enjoy your date with Luke tomorrow."

He waved to Lenny who was watching them from the window, then marched off toward his truck.

Back inside, Lenny was sitting at his desk, grinning from ear to ear. "Didn't freeze to death, I see."

"Not even close," Hannah said, cheeks still tingling from the cold—or maybe from laughing so much.

Alyssa waited exactly three seconds before popping her head around the corner. "So?"

"So what?"

"So how was it? Did he kiss you? Did he pledge his undying love?"

Hannah rolled her eyes. "He brought cookies."

"That's a yes, then."

Hannah ignored her, but as she went back to her desk, she caught a glimpse of her reflection in the window. She looked happy. Flushed, a little windblown, but happy.

Her phone buzzed again.

Carter may have wildflowers, but
I've got something waiting
tomorrow night that is twice as
sweet and totally edible.

As Hannah tucked her phone away and pulled out the stack of subscription renewals, she couldn't help but feel a little giddy. If this was what pretending felt like, then the next few weeks were going to be a whole lot of fun.

Ten

HANNAH

HANNAH STOOD in front of her bedroom mirror, smoothing the wrinkles from her green sweater. She tucked a wayward curl behind her ear and stepped back to assess the full effect. Dark jeans, an emerald sweater that matched the green in her eyes, and her favorite leather boots. Casual but nice. Perfect for her first official "date" with Luke.

The sound of tires on the driveway reminded her what time it was. Hannah peeked through the curtains to see Luke's red truck, its headlights briefly illuminating her small front porch. The doorbell rang, and Hannah gave herself one final glance in the mirror before skipping down the stairs and opening her door.

Luke stood on her doorstep, his quiet charisma on full display despite the simple clothes—clean jeans, work boots, and a button-down shirt that looked like he'd actually ironed it. As he stepped inside, she caught the subtle scent of aftershave. Not Ben's leather-and-spice, but still, something nice.

"Well, well, well," he said."Look how pretty you look!"

She felt her cheeks grow warm under his attention. "Thanks. You clean up pretty nicely yourself, Dr. Merriwether."

He nodded. "Special occasion. Not every day I get to take the most popular woman in Bluestem out to dinner."

Hannah rolled her eyes, but couldn't help smiling. "Is that what I am now? The most popular woman in town?"

"According to Lenny, who cornered me at the feed store this afternoon." Luke laughed. "He wanted to know if I was aware that you'd had lunch with Carter Manchester in the town square yesterday."

Hannah groaned. "Of course he did."

"I told him I was well aware, and that I had plans of my own for you tonight. Something a little more romantic than a sack lunch on a cold park bench." Luke held out his arm with an exaggerated flourish. "Shall we show Bluestem what a proper date looks like?"

Hannah slipped her arm through his, playing along. "Absolutely."

The night air was crisp as they walked to the truck. Luke opened the passenger door for her and waited until she'd buckled her seatbelt before circling around and getting in himself.

"So what exactly did you tell Lenny about tonight?" she asked.

Luke's grin was visible in the glow of the dashboard lights. "That I was taking you somewhere Carter couldn't possibly compete with. Somewhere that would make his picnic look like amateur hour."

"Are you going to tell me where we're going, or do I have to guess?"

He shot her a sideways glance, eyes gleaming in the dark. "We're going to the Rusty Spur. Wyatt's got a table set up for us."

Hannah laughed. "The Rusty Spur is going to make Carter's picnic look like amateur hour?"

"Just wait and see."

Trucks and cars packed the parking lot. "Busy night," she said as Luke maneuvered his truck into one of the few remaining spaces.

"Mm-hmm," he murmured, his tone suspiciously noncommittal.

She turned to Luke, eyebrows raised. "Just how public is this date going to be?"

Luke cut the engine and turned toward her, his expression both apologetic and excited. "Well, let's just say that by tomorrow morning, there won't be a single person in Bluestem who doesn't know you had a date with Luke Merriwether tonight."

Hannah's stomach did a little flip. *Including Ben?*

Luke must have seen her reaction, because he took her hand, his touch warm and steady. "This will be fun. I promise. Just you and me, having dinner at the Rusty Spur. In front of some of our neighbors and friends."

Hannah took a deep breath. "Okay. If you say so."

They walked toward the entrance together, and Hannah felt a flutter of nerves as Luke's hand settled on the small of her back. Wyatt was waiting for them, just inside the door, wearing a white shirt and an actual bow tie, something she'd never seen him wear in all her years of coming to the Rusty Spur.

"Madam. Sir. Your table is prepared." He kept his voice low and grave, but the corners of his mouth twitched with barely contained laughter. "If you'll follow me."

Luke tipped his hat toward Wyatt and extended his arm to Hannah. She slipped her hand into the crook of his elbow, and Wyatt led them through the main dining area, where neighbors and friends sat at the scarred wooden tables, some pausing mid-bite to stare as Hannah and Luke passed. The usual plastic baskets of burgers and fries dotted the tables, alongside mason jars filled with beer or soda. Everything was exactly as it always was—except for the way every eye in the place followed their progress across the room.

Wyatt paused at a corner table covered in an ironed white tablecloth that looked startlingly out of place among the rustic wooden furnishings. A slender vase held a single red rose, and a flickering candle cast a golden glow over folded cloth napkins, gleaming silverware, and glass wine goblets.

"Your table, Madam," Wyatt said, pulling out a chair with another dramatic flourish.

She glanced across the room and spotted Riley and Alyssa, tucked into a booth with a perfect view. Riley had a grin so wide it threatened to split his face, and Alyssa was holding up her phone, ready to document every romantic moment.

Hannah grinned and took her seat, feeling like the star of a quirky romcom, surrounded by an audience of familiar faces, all eager to witness the charming performance of an exaggerated dinner date.

Wyatt produced two hand-written menus, each inked in a swirling script that looked suspiciously like Mrs. K.'s perfect penmanship. "Tonight," Wyatt announced, loud enough for at least half the restaurant to hear, "our chef has prepared a special menu for our distinguished guests. We begin with a delicate salad of mixed greens, followed by the chef's signature pasta. This will be followed by a decadent dessert, all prepared by the legendary Mrs. K."

Luke took his menu and pretended to study it. "You had me at decadent."

"I recommend the house wine," Wyatt continued, gesturing to a carafe already chilling in an ice bucket on their table. "A fine vintage... from last month's delivery."

Hannah nearly choked on her water, coughing as she tried not to laugh.

Luke reached over and patted her back gently. "Easy there," he murmured, his eyes dancing with amusement. "We haven't even started yet."

Wyatt filled their wine goblets with ceremonial solemnity and then, with a wink at Hannah, inclined his head, collected the menus, and vanished toward the kitchen.

As soon as he was gone, Hannah leaned across the table. "I can't believe you did all this," she said, her voice filled with wonder.

Luke set his hat on the chair next to him and leaned back, looking smug. "I only asked him to reserve us a table, and fix us something special for supper. Wyatt and his mom did the rest."

Hannah looked across the room. "And let me guess—Alyssa is the official event photographer?"

"Strictly candid shots, I'm told," Luke said. "She promised to only post the best ones."

Hannah groaned and took in the scene. The other diners tried—unsuccessfully—to look like they weren't staring, but she caught at least three people openly whispering behind their menus. One of them was Mrs. Peterson, who sat with her husband and another couple at a table by the wall. Her fork hovered halfway to her mouth, forgotten, as she watched Hannah and Luke with undisguised interest.

Hannah picked up her wineglass and took a careful sip, trying to focus on the tart sweetness instead of the weight of all those watchful eyes.

"You okay?" Luke asked, his voice low enough that only she could hear. "You're gripping that glass pretty tight."

She studied his face—the genuine concern in his brown eyes, the way his shoulders had tensed slightly as he waited for her answer. Luke really was trying to make their date seem real. The least she could do was appreciate the effort.

She nodded, setting down the glass. "Just realizing that Carter's picnic seems downright private compared to this."

"That's the point." Luke's grin widened.

"Besides, I had to up the ante. He brought you flowers *and* took you to the hitching bench."

"It's just... everyone's staring."

Luke leaned forward, his voice dropping to a conspiratorial whisper. "That's exactly what we wanted, remember? To give them something to talk about." His eyes crinkled at the corners as his smile widened.

"Then it's a total success." Hannah raised her wineglass in a small toast. "Here's to our not-so-private dinner date."

Luke clinked his glass against hers. "May it be memorable for all the right reasons."

Across the room, Alyssa raised her phone for another photo, and this time, Hannah stuck out her tongue for the camera.

Wyatt returned with two small salads, each artfully arranged on white plates that Hannah had never seen at the Rusty Spur before. "Your first course," he announced, setting them down with precision. "Enjoy."

The salad looked delicious, with candied walnuts and slices of apple nestled among the greens. She took a bite of her salad, surprised by the tangy sweetness of the dressing. "I had no idea Mrs. K. could make something this fancy."

Wyatt grinned. "She dug out her Julia Child cookbook just for the occasion."

As if summoned by the mere mention of her name, Mrs. K. emerged from the kitchen, her face flushed with pride as she carried two steaming plates toward their table. She'd swapped her usual apron for a crisp black one and pinned a small artificial flower to her collar—another touch that made this evening feel surreal. The rich aroma of garlic and herbs reached Hannah before the plates did, making her mouth water despite her lingering embarrassment.

"Homemade fettuccine," Mrs. K. announced, setting the plates down with a flourish that mimicked Wyatt's exaggerated formality. "

Hannah looked down at her plate. Fresh Parmesan and sprigs of herbs dusted the artfully arranged pasta. "This looks amazing," she said, inhaling the fragrant steam. "Thank you, Mrs. K."

The older woman beamed with pride, and retreated toward the kitchen. As the swinging door closed behind her, soft music began playing from the speakers. Not the usual classic rock or country that typically filled the Rusty Spur, but something slow and romantic. She recognized the melody immediately: **At Last** by Etta James.

"Did you plan that too?" she asked.

Luke smiled. "Alyssa may have sent me a playlist."

Hannah glanced across the room at Alyssa, who raised her glass in a silent toast.

Hannah raised her glass in return and mouthed a silent "thank you". Alyssa beamed and snapped another photo.

Hannah twirled her fork into the pasta, savoring the first bite. The flavors were rich and complex. She closed her eyes for a moment, letting herself enjoy the food despite the many eyes watching her.

"Good?" Luke asked, his voice warm and rich like the pasta sauce.

"Heavenly," she said.

"I may not have Carter's greenhouse connections, but I know people who know their way around a kitchen," Luke said.

Hannah laughed, relaxing into the absurdity of the situation. The music shifted to another of her favorites: **The Way You Look Tonight.** Her chest tightened. Of course, Alyssa would pick the most romantic song in existence.

Wyatt cleared their dishes, and Mrs. K. returned with two slices of cheesecake. Generous mounds of whipped cream crowned each slice, with raspberry sauce drizzling down the sides. "My own secret recipe," she said, setting the plates before them.

Hannah smiled. "That meal was amazing, Mrs. K. And now cheesecake? You went above and beyond for us. Thank you."

Mrs. K. blushed, her cheeks pink with pleasure. "Well, it's not every day we get to host such a romantic evening. You two enjoy every bite." Mrs. K. gave their shoulders each a pat, then turned and bustled back toward the kitchen, her black apron strings bouncing with each step.

Hannah watched her go and felt a flutter of gratitude mixed with something deeper. They'd gone to so much trouble—not just Luke, but Carter and Alyssa and Wyatt and Mrs. K. too—creating these absurd romantic dates just for her. Just to help her feel better about making a fool of herself on New Year's Eve.

"Thank you," she said, smiling at Luke over the flickering candlelight. "For everything. The flowers and the picnic with Carter yesterday and now... this ridiculous, wonderful dinner. I needed it more than I realized."

"You're welcome. And I'm glad it helped. You seem... happier tonight. More like your old self."

"I am happier," Hannah said. "Who knew the Rusty Spur could be so romantic? So, what's next?"

Luke cocked his head, considered his answer, then smiled. "You and me and Carter keep giving them something to talk about."

Hannah laughed. "Sounds perfect." She took a bite of the dessert, closing her eyes as the creamy sweetness melted on her tongue. "Although not as perfect as this cheesecake. It is incredible!"

Luke grinned and took his own bite, nodding in agreement. "Mrs. K. outdid herself."

Hannah savored another forkful, letting the sweetness linger. The candlelight flickered between them, casting dancing shadows across the white tablecloth. When Wyatt brought the check—tucked inside a small leather folder with exaggerated ceremony—Luke insisted on paying despite Hannah's protests.

"My idea, my treat," he said firmly. "Besides,

if Carter heard you paid for our meal, I'd never hear the end of it."

They stood to leave, and Hannah felt every eye in the restaurant follow them again. Mrs. Peterson actually waved as they passed, and Riley gave Luke an enthusiastic thumbs-up from across the room.

When they pulled into her driveway, Luke walked her to the door but didn't kiss her—they both knew this wasn't that kind of date—but he did pull her into a hug. "Sleep well, Hannah Banana," he said, then jogged back to his truck.

She watched his taillights disappear down the road, then let herself into the quiet house. The hallway mirror reflected her flushed cheeks and bright eyes—the picture of a woman who'd just had a wonderful night on the town.

And as she climbed the stairs to her room, she couldn't stop herself from pulling out her phone and scrolling through Alyssa's social media posts. There they were: photos of her and Luke at their candlelit table, laughing over their fancy dinner at the Rusty Spur. The comments were already rolling in—friends and neighbors weighing in on how cute they looked together, how romantic the whole thing was.

She set the phone down and stared at her reflection in the bedroom mirror. The same green sweater, the same girl. But something in her eyes looked different now. Uncertain. Searching.

"What are you doing, Hannah?" she whispered to her reflection.

The girl in the mirror didn't answer. She just stared back, her expression caught somewhere between hope and heartache, still wanting something she couldn't quite name.

Eleven

BEN

Ben stared at the verse in his open Bible, the words blurring before his eyes as the morning sunlight streamed through the windows at Daisy's Diner. The Tenth Commandment, *Thou shalt not covet*, stared back at him accusingly. His coffee had grown cold, sermon notes scattered across the table like fallen leaves, his thoughts as scattered as the papers.

Every time he tried to focus, his mind wandered back to Hannah Mitchell. That wild, curly red hair. The hazel flecks in her green eyes. Those lips that had touched his for only seconds but had somehow burrowed themselves into his memory with startling permanence.

He tapped his pen against the yellow legal

pad, where he'd written only three words: "Coveting vs. Admiring." Not exactly a compelling sermon title. He'd already covered "New Beginnings" last Sunday, and while the congregation had responded well, he needed something different this week. And he'd opted for something that might help him process his own tangled emotions.

Ben took another sip of his lukewarm coffee and grimaced. Just as he raised his hand to signal the waitress for a refill, a burst of laughter erupted from the table behind him.

"I'm telling you, Carter had a whole picnic set up in the gazebo!" a woman's voice said. "In January! With a portable heater and everything."

"That Manchester boy never does anything halfway," another voice chimed in. "I heard he sent Hannah flowers, too. In January!"

Ben's hand froze mid-air.

Ben slowly lowered his hand, suddenly no longer interested in fresh coffee. He straightened his collar. The physical reminder of his position felt particularly heavy just then.

"Where did they go after lunch?" the first voice asked.

"Back to the Gazette, I suppose. But then I

heard she had a date with Luke Merriwether the very next night."

"Both of them? In one week?"

Ben stared down at his notes, pretending to concentrate, but his ears strained to catch every word. His pencil pressed so hard against the paper that the tip broke, leaving a slight bruise on "Admiring."

He exhaled slowly and reached for a fresh pencil from his bag. "Thou shalt not covet," he whispered to himself. The irony wasn't lost on him.

The bell above the door jingled, and a rush of cold air swept in. Ben glanced up to see Lenny and Hattie Beckett enter the diner, stomping snow from their boots.

"Lenny. Hattie. Over here," the woman behind him called. "We've got plenty of room."

"Morning, Pastor," Lenny said as he passed Ben's table, his voice carrying through the diner.

"Good morning, Lenny, Hattie. How are you both today?"

"Can't complain," Lenny said, tipping his worn cap. "Looks like you're working on our next message."

Ben nodded. "Trying to, at least. Not making much progress."

Hattie gave him a warm smile. "Don't let us interrupt your sermon writing, Pastor. We know Sunday comes whether you're ready or not."

Ben returned her smile, grateful for the understanding. "That it does."

Hattie and Lenny moved on, and Ben heard chairs scraping against the linoleum floor as they settled at the table behind him.

"So, Lenny," the woman's voice dropped to a conspiratorial whisper that was still perfectly audible to Ben, "is it true what they're saying? Hannah Mitchell is dating both Carter Manchester and Luke Merriwether? At the same time?"

"Now, you know I'm not one to gossip," Lenny said, not bothering to lower his voice. "But that's sort of what it looks like. One day, Carter is bringing her flowers and taking her out for a picnic lunch. Then the next day, Luke is inviting her to the Rusty Spur for dinner."

"Did you see the pictures Alyssa posted?" Hattie asked. "Candlelight, white tablecloth, the works. Luke must have paid Wyatt and his mom a pretty penny to do all that. I've never seen the Rusty Spur look so fancy!"

Ben ran a hand through his hair and tried to ignore their carrying voices. This was exactly what small towns did—they gossiped. It wasn't personal. But he couldn't deny the sharp twist in his stomach at the image of Hannah laughing across a candlelit table with Luke Merriwether. Or strolling through the town square with Carter Manchester and his picnic basket.

"Refill, Pastor?"

Ben startled and looked up to find the waitress, coffeepot in hand, smiling down at him.

"Yes, please. Thank you." The coffee tasted bitter when he sipped it. He set the mug down and stared at the Bible verse again, trying to find inspiration for his sermon. But all he could see was Hannah's face when she'd opened his office door and recognized him—the shock and mortification in those expressive eyes.

Ben stared down at his fragmented notes, knowing it was useless to continue. The diner hummed with conversations—some about the weather, others about the upcoming festival, but too many about Hannah and her dates. Each word felt like a pebble dropping into the still pond of his concentration, rippling outward, disrupting his thoughts.

He closed his Bible with a quiet thud and began packing his things. The sermon wouldn't come here, not with every other table discussing the very woman he was trying *not* to think about.

As he stepped outside into the sharp January air, Ben pulled his coat tighter around him and gazed up at the clear blue sky. The cold clarity felt good after the stuffy warmth of the diner. Maybe that's what he needed—some clear thinking about Hannah Mitchell, and his place in her life. Which was as her pastor. Nothing more, at least for the next three months.

THE LATE AFTERNOON sun slanted through the lace curtains of Ben's room at the Whitemore, casting long shadows across his desk. His Bible lay open to Exodus. Outside, Main Street hummed with the quiet rhythm of small-town life, but inside, Ben's thoughts were anything but quiet.

The Tenth Commandment was straightforward enough: don't desire what belongs to your neighbor. Don't covet his house, his wife, his possessions. It was meant to guard the heart against the kind of envy that turned neighbor against neighbor, friend against friend.

Ben stood up and walked to the window, watching as the setting sun painted Bluestem's storefronts in shades of amber and gold. A few shops were already closed for the night, but Daisy's Diner glowed with warm light, and further down, he could see the illuminated sign of the Rusty Spur. The Rusty Spur, where Hannah and Luke had shared that candlelit dinner everyone was talking about. The thought sent a familiar twist of something uncomfortable through his chest.

"It's better this way," he told his reflection in the window glass. The clear boundaries created by her dating someone—or apparently, two someones—were a blessing in disguise. There could be no confusion about appropriate behavior now, no lingering questions about that midnight kiss.

Ben turned away from his reflection and back to his notes. What would his congregation need to hear about coveting? What wisdom could he offer them when he was struggling with the very same issue?

Perhaps that was precisely the point. Maybe his own internal battle was exactly what made him qualified to speak on the subject.

He picked up his pen and began to write, the words coming more freely now: "Wanting what we cannot have is part of the human condition. From the Garden of Eden to the present day, we've struggled with the gap between what is and what we desire."

He continued, pen moving steadily across the page: "The Tenth Commandment isn't about shutting down all desire—it's about recognizing when our desires become destructive, when wanting turns into coveting what rightfully belongs to another."

Ben paused, pondering his next words carefully. "But what about desires that don't infringe on others' rights? What about longing for something that simply isn't meant for us? The Bible offers guidance here too."

His pen moved faster now, the sermon taking shape beneath his hand. He would talk about Paul, pleading three times for relief from his thorn in the flesh, only to hear 'My grace is sufficient.' About Moses, standing on Mount Nebo, gazing at the Promised Land he would never enter. About Jeremiah, commanded by God to remain single and childless in a culture where family was everything. About desires that were pure and personal, yet denied for a greater purpose.

And maybe, if he was brave enough, he would touch on the hardest lesson of all—learning to rejoice in others' happiness, even when it highlighted what you lacked.

The light outside had faded completely now, leaving only the reflection of his lamp in the window glass. Ben's gaze drifted to his phone, lying silent on the nightstand. How easy it would be to invent some question about the Winter Festival, some excuse to call Hannah. To hear her voice, to reassure himself that their professional relationship remained intact despite the awkwardness between them.

He pushed the thought away and turned back to his sermon notes. This was exactly the kind of thinking his sermon needed to address—the subtle ways coveting crept in, disguising itself as innocent concern or professional interest.

"The antidote to coveting," he wrote, "is not the absence of desire, but the presence of gratitude. When we focus on what we have rather than what we lack, we find contentment even in the midst of unfulfilled desires."

Ben sat back, studying what he'd written. The sermon was taking shape, becoming something that might actually help his congregation—and himself. A roadmap for navigating the territory between wanting and coveting, between healthy desire and destructive envy.

He glanced at his reflection once more in the darkened window. The frown had eased from his brow, replaced by a look of quiet determination. He couldn't change the fact that Hannah Mitchell was dating other men. He couldn't undo their awkward history or the complications created by his role as pastor.

But he could choose how to respond to those realities. He could choose to be the pastor Bluestem needed, even if it meant setting aside what the man, Ben Landry, wanted.

With renewed purpose, Ben turned back to his sermon notes. By Sunday, he would have something worth saying about desire and contentment—something that might help others walking similar paths. And maybe, in the process of writing it, he would finally make peace with his own complicated feelings.

Outside, snow blurred the streetlights into halos. Ben set down his pen and leaned forward, elbows on the desk, the lamplight pooling around him. "Lord," he whispered, "teach me to want what You want—to be content with the path You've laid before me."

His throat tightened around the next words. "Even when I can't see where that path leads. Even when it feels like I'm walking blindfolded through the forest."

The words fell into the quiet like a confession, and for the first time all day, he let the silence answer.

Twelve

HANNAH

HANNAH PULLED into the church parking lot fifteen minutes early. Her heart hammered against her ribs as she forced herself to turn off the engine. Adjusting the strap of her bag, she climbed out of her old Subaru and reminded herself that if she could survive a week of dates with Carter and Luke, she could handle anything the Festival committee might throw at her.

Mrs. Peterson was already there, arranging lemon bars, paper cups, and a coffee carafe at the refreshment table, her pencil tucked behind her ear as always. "Hannah! You're early," she said, waving her over. "I have the snacks ready and waiting."

"Good evening, Mrs. Peterson." Hannah set

her bag on a folding chair. "Did you have a chance to review the agenda I emailed yesterday?"

Mrs. Peterson gave a dismissive flap of her hand. "Of course I did. I even printed three copies—one for you, one for me, and one for Pastor Ben." She straightened her glasses, eyes darting to the door as it opened behind them. "He'll be joining us later, if he has time. He's finishing up a phone call."

Hannah's smile froze slightly at the mention of Ben, but she nodded. "Great." She moved to the head table and began arranging her notes, pretending to focus on the task at hand, while anxiously monitoring the door. It wasn't nerves, exactly—just a sixth sense that warned her trouble was headed her way.

And right on time, trouble arrived. At exactly 6:57, Carter Manchester strode in, carrying two travel mugs, with that signature cowboy swagger that made half the women in town go weak in the knees. His sandy hair was perfectly tousled, and his broad shoulders filled out his denim jacket like he'd stepped off a ranch calendar.

"Hello, Darling!" Carter said, as if he'd been

attending these meetings with her every month for the past two months. "Hope I'm not late."

Hannah stared, dumbstruck, as Carter made a show of scanning the room for empty seats before joining her at the head table.

He set the two mugs down in front of him and bent close, voice pitched low. "I brought you hot cocoa," he said, sliding one toward Hannah. "From Daisy's. None of the Mrs. Peterson's motor oil for my gal."

Before she could react, the door opened again, and in walked Luke—button-down shirt, blue jeans, and a leather-bound notebook tucked under one arm. He circled the room, greeting each of the committee members by name, before joining Hannah and Luke at the front table.

Hannah found her voice. "You're both here for the Festival committee meeting?"

"Wouldn't miss it," Carter said, smiling at her adoringly.

"Same," Luke added. "It's important to you, so it's important to me."

"Did you two lose a bet?" Clayton asked, eyebrows raised.

"No bet, Mr. Lesiak," Carter said. "We're just

here to help Hannah make this the best Winter Festival this town has ever seen."

Mrs. Peterson practically vibrated with excitement. "Well, this is just wonderful!" she said, clapping her hands together. "In all my years as church secretary, I've never seen two young men volunteer for Festival planning. Looks like we should have made Hannah our chair years ago!"

Ruby Carhart leaned forward, squinting at the two men through her thick glasses. "Are you boys planning to actually help, or are you just here to look pretty?"

Carter grinned at Ruby, his charm turned up to full voltage. "Oh, we're here to help, Mrs. Carhart. Hannah's got us completely wrapped around her little finger."

Luke nodded solemnly. "It's true. We're at her beck and call."

Hannah felt heat creep up her neck as several committee members exchanged knowing looks. She tried to regain her composure, flipping briskly through her notes. This was her committee, her meeting, and she refused to let Carter and Luke's unexpected appearance throw her off track.

"Well, um, thank you both for volunteering," she managed. "Let's get started, shall we?"

She glanced around the room, doing a quick headcount. Twelve people, including Carter and Luke. Their presence was a distraction she hadn't expected, and the empty chair at the end of the table was a distraction she couldn't ignore. Maybe running away to California would have been the simpler choice, after all.

Thirteen

BEN

Ben ended his call with the district superintendent and checked his watch. The Festival planning meeting had started fifteen minutes ago. He tucked his phone into his pocket and quickened his pace down the empty church hallway, his footsteps echoing against the polished floor. He'd wanted to be there from the beginning, to show support for Hannah and the committee. But church business was church business, and some calls couldn't wait. Especially when they were from his boss.

He paused outside the Fellowship Hall, taking a deep breath. Through the small window in the door, he could see a dozen or more volunteers—more attendees than he'd expected for a midweek planning meeting. Ben eased the door open and slipped inside, grateful when no one turned to look. He found an empty chair at a back table and settled in quietly, not wanting to interrupt.

From his vantage point, Ben had a clear view of Hannah at the front table. Her wild, red curls caught the fluorescent light as she gestured toward a large easel with what appeared to be a hand-drawn diagram of the church grounds. She was flanked by two men Ben recognized immediately—Carter Manchester and Luke Merriwether.

"As you can see," Hannah was saying, her voice clear and confident, "I've mapped out the traditional booths along the south walkway. Mrs. Peterson has the sign-up sheets for volunteers."

Carter leaned forward, his enthusiasm practically radiating from him. "But what if we moved everything to create a central plaza effect?" He jumped up and strode to the easel, turning the page to reveal a blank sheet. He grabbed a marker and began sketching with broad, sweeping strokes. "Imagine walking in beneath an archway of twinkling lights, with vintage-style lanterns illuminating your path all the way to the heart of the festival. Then, here in the middle, a circular arrangement with all the food vendors, and radiating out from there, the game booths and craft displays."

Ben watched as Hannah's expression shifted from surprise to polite interest. She didn't seem annoyed by the interruption, merely patient—as if she'd been expecting something like this.

"And over here," Carter continued, his marker squeaking against the paper, "we could set up horse-drawn carriage rides circling the entire festival area." He spun around and faced the committee. "Think about it! Kids bundled up in blankets, hot chocolate in their mittened hands, the rhythmic clip-clop of hooves on the path!" His enthusiasm was infectious. Several committee members nodded appreciatively, and even Hannah smiled.

But Luke was already shaking his head, tapping his pen against his notebook. "Carter, those carriages would need a track at least eight feet wide. That would cut into the space for the booths by almost thirty percent if they stayed on the church grounds."

He stood and joined Carter at the easel,

taking the marker from him. "What if, instead, we had the carriage rides take a quick tour of the town? Visitors could see the holiday lights downtown and come back refreshed. And for something special right here, a family portrait station with a winter backdrop—professional quality photos at a reasonable price, all proceeds to the church, of course."

Carter crossed his arms, considering. "Not bad, Merriwether. But where's the magic? The spectacle?" He took the marker back, adding a flourish to Luke's neat diagram. "What about an ice-carving demonstration? We could bring in that guy from Kearney who did the sculptures for the Manchester Trucking Christmas party last year."

"That would certainly draw a crowd," Luke said. "But we'd need to consider the logistics. Electric outlets for his tools, drainage for the melting ice, safety barriers to keep curious kids from getting too close..."

Ben leaned back in his chair, fascinated by the drama unfolding before him. Hannah stood slightly to the side now, watching Carter and Luke with an expression somewhere between mingled amusement and resignation. The committee members chuckled at their back-and-forth, clearly entertained.

Finally, Hannah stepped forward and reclaimed her position at the easel. "Thank you, Guys," she said. "These are all excellent ideas, but perhaps we should get through the basic agenda before we redesign the entire festival?"

Carter and Luke exchanged a look that Ben couldn't quite interpret.

"Of course, Hannah," Carter said, settling back into his chair. "You're the boss."

Luke nodded solemnly. "We're just here to support your vision."

Hannah rolled her eyes, but there was warmth in the gesture. "As I was saying before I was so enthusiastically interrupted..." She flipped back to her original diagram. "Mrs. Peterson has the volunteer sign-up sheets. We'll need at least thirty people to run the booths, plus additional help for set-up and clean-up."

As the meeting continued, Ben paid less attention to the festival details and more attention to the interplay between Hannah and her two enthusiastic helpers. There was something about their interactions he couldn't quite place —a rhythm that felt well-practiced, almost choreographed. Carter would make a grandiose suggestion, Luke would temper it with practicality, and Hannah would find the middle ground with the patience of Job.

The pattern continued as they discussed games for the children's area. Carter proposed an elaborate snow maze with tunnels and ice slides. Luke pointed out potential safety hazards and the liability issues. Then, while Hannah was considering alternatives, Carter nudged Luke's elbow and murmured something that made the veterinarian's lips twitch with suppressed laughter.

Even more telling was Hannah's reaction to them. When Carter leaned close to point something out on her notes, she didn't blush or get flustered. When Luke's hand briefly touched hers as they exchanged a pen, there was no lingering glance or shy smile. She treated each of them with the comfortable familiarity of a longtime friend. Nothing more.

"Now, about the decorations," Hannah said. "We've used the same winter theme for years, but I was thinking we could refresh it."

"What about a Northern Lights theme?" Carter asked. "Deep blues, purples, green accent lighting. We could hang those icicle lights from the ceiling in patterns."

For once, Luke nodded in agreement. "That could work. Dramatic but not too complicated."

Hannah's smile brightened. "I love that idea. Mrs. Peterson, could you add that to the notes?"

As Mrs. Peterson jotted something down, Ben observed the quick flash of triumph that passed between Carter and Luke—a shared victory rather than individual accomplishment.

The realization sent a wave of relief through Ben's chest, loosening a knot he hadn't fully realized was there. Whatever game the three of them were playing at—this "competition" for Hannah's attention—it was just that: a game. One they all seemed to be in on.

But why the charade? Why would Hannah encourage two men to pretend to compete for her affection? Ben's mind circled back to New Year's Eve. Hannah's soft lips pressed against his under the mistletoe. The warmth of her waist beneath his hand. The fleeting but unmistakable connection he'd felt in that moment—followed immediately by the horror in her eyes when she'd realized what she'd done.

Then there was that mortifying moment in

his office when she'd discovered who he really was. The color had drained from her face so quickly he'd worried she might faint. Her folder had slipped from her fingers, papers scattering across the floor as she'd stammered apologies, unable to even look him in the eye.

Now these elaborate public dates with Carter and Luke. The pieces slowly fell into place. They were creating a distraction, giving the town something to talk about besides Hannah kissing the new pastor on New Year's Eve. And from the interested looks on the committee members' faces whenever Carter or Luke spoke, it was working beautifully.

Ben found himself fighting a smile. Hannah's friends were shielding the both of them from gossip by creating a more entertaining story. There was something deeply touching about Carter and Luke's willingness to make themselves the center of attention—all to protect Hannah from potential embarrassment over one impulsive moment.

And that, Ben had to admit, only made her more intriguing.

"Before we wrap up," Hannah said, drawing Ben's attention back to the meeting, "let's review our action items for next week." She glanced down at her notes. "Mrs. Peterson will coordinate the volunteer schedule. Ruby and Clayton will handle the silent auction donations. Carter and Luke have generously offered to work on the Northern Lights decorations." Her eyes crinkled with amusement. "Though I suspect we'll end up with something resembling a rodeo in space if I don't supervise closely."

The committee chuckled, and Carter clutched his chest in mock offense. "I'm wounded, Hannah. Truly wounded."

"You'll survive," she replied, her tone warm with affection. "Now, does anyone have questions before we adjourn?"

Ruby raised her hand. "Will Pastor Ben be available to help with the planning, too? Pastor John always assisted with the Festival."

All heads turned toward the back of the room.

"I'm happy to help in any way I can," Ben said, offering a smile to the room and ending with Hannah. "Pastor John shared his notes on the Festival before he left, and I'm looking forward to being part of this annual tradition."

Hannah's expression softened slightly.

"Thank you, Pastor Ben," she said, her voice steady and professional. "We appreciate your support."

For a moment, their eyes held, and Ben felt something quiet pass between them—not embarrassment or awkwardness as he might have expected, but a simple acknowledgment. A recognition that she might be truly ready to move forward from that New Year's Eve moment with grace, rather than continued discomfort.

"That concludes our meeting," Hannah announced, gathering her papers into a neat stack. "Thank you all for coming. Same time next week."

The committee members rose, chatting in small groups as they put on coats and collected purses. Ben stood, intending to make his way toward Hannah, perhaps offer a word of praise for how well she'd managed the meeting. But before he could take more than two steps, Carter and Luke had flanked her like sentinels, efficiently gathering her materials and guiding her toward the door.

"Late night snack at Daisy's?" he heard Carter ask. "I'm starving after all that creative planning."

"You're always starving," Luke said, helping Hannah into her coat with practiced ease.

"Because I work harder than you, Doc," Carter shot back, hoisting Hannah's bag onto his shoulder despite her protests.

Hannah laughed, shaking her head at their antics as the three of them moved as a unit toward the exit.

Ben watched them go, making no effort to intercept them. Instead, he gathered his own notes and nodded farewell to Mrs. Peterson. As he switched off the lights, Ben realized, for the first time since arriving in Bluestem, he truly felt at peace with where he was. Not just geographically, but emotionally.

He moved through the darkened church with sure steps, his hand brushing lightly against the wall. It struck him that faith—and love—often meant finding your way slowly, one careful step at a time.

Outside, the January air was crisp and still. The Nebraska sky stretched vast and clear above him, stars scattered like snowflakes against the dark. His grandmother had always said that God rarely rushed, but He was never late.

Ben smiled, turning his coat collar up against

the cold as he walked to his car. Whatever was unfolding between Hannah and him would reveal itself in its own time—he didn't need to force it. For tonight, it was enough to know that the path ahead, though uncertain, no longer felt quite so crowded.

Fourteen

HANNAH

HANNAH PUSHED OPEN the door to the Gazette office, the familiar scent of ink and paper greeting her. She'd been up since dawn, finalizing details for the Winter Festival that was fast approaching. Between that and navigating Luke and Carter's increasingly elaborate "dates," she was running on caffeine and determination.

"Morning, Lenny," she called to the typesetter hunched over his desk. "Please tell me the flyers are ready."

Lenny Beckett looked up, his weathered face breaking into a grin. "Just finished the last batch." He gestured to a neat stack of colorful papers. "Came out real nice, if I say so myself."

Hannah crossed the room and picked one up,

admiring the crisp layout and vibrant design. "These look fantastic. Mrs. K. has a committee that is going to post them around town today, if I can get them to the Rusty Spur before noon."

Lenny pushed back from his desk, his chair squeaking in protest "Before you head to the Spur, there's something I need to talk to you about."

Hannah paused, flyers in hand. "If it's about the festival coverage, Alyssa said the article would be ready later today."

"It's not about the festival. Well, not directly." Lenny gestured to the chair beside his desk. "This won't take long, but you might want to sit down."

Hannah sighed but complied, her curiosity piqued. "What's going on?"

Lenny leaned forward, lowering his voice despite the empty office. "Wyatt's gone and started himself a pool."

"A pool?" Hannah's brow furrowed. "What kind of a pool?"

"A Valentine's Day pool on which of those two Romeos of yours are going to be your date for Valentine's Day." Lenny's eyes twinkled with barely contained amusement. "Got two big jars behind the counter and everything. Five dollars gets folks a guess on whether you'll pick Luke or Carter."

Hannah's jaw dropped. "You're joking."

"Nope." Lenny shook his head. "Ruby Carhart put her money on Luke—says a woman your age needs stability, not flash. But the Frasier twins both went for Carter. Something about his smile." He shrugged. "Wyatt's even got charts showing which of those two cowboys has raised the most money so far."

Hannah's embarrassment shifted, morphing into something hotter and sharper. Her jaw clenched so tight she could feel a dull ache spreading through her temples. "People are betting on my love life?"

"It's all in good fun," Lenny said, patting her arm. "I put my money on Luke, by the way. That dinner he arranged was mighty impressive."

Hannah barely heard him. Her mind raced through the implications. "How long has this been going on?"

"About a week," Lenny said. "Started small, just the regulars. But word spread."

Hannah stood abruptly, her chair rolling

backward. "Thanks for the heads-up, Lenny," she said, her voice tight. "I appreciate it."

Her hands shook with rage as she tucked the flyers into her bag, then headed to the door, her mind already rehearsing exactly what she planned to say to Wyatt Kepler when she found him.

THE RUSTY SPUR was quieter than usual for a Friday afternoon, with just a handful of regulars scattered throughout the place. A few farmers in their good boots and ball caps occupied the front tables, arguing over the new cattle tax.

At the bar, the usual suspects huddled around the battered wood, chatting over popcorn and beer. Wyatt moved behind the counter with his typical unhurried efficiency, pulling tap handles and filling glasses.

Hannah marched up to the bar, each step fueled by a mixture of embarrassment and indignation. The Rusty Spur's Friday patrons parted before her like she was Moses approaching the Red Sea—probably because the look on her face was enough to make even the rowdiest cowboy think twice about getting in her way.

Wyatt glanced up from the draft beer he was pouring, his eyes widening slightly as he registered her expression. He finished the pour with a practiced flick of his wrist, handed it to a waiting customer, and turned to face her with a smile that was equal parts charm and caution.

"Mitchell," he said, his voice pitched low and friendly. "You're just the person I wanted to see."

"Don't you Mitchell me," she said. "We need to talk. Now." She slammed her bag onto the counter, and several of the flyers slid out and landed on the floor. A few heads at the bar turned, then quickly turned away, like prairie dogs spotting a hawk.

Wyatt put both hands on the bar, giving her his full attention. "You're here about the pool, I'm guessing." His smile faltered for just a second before he recovered. "I was going to mention that to you."

Hannah's glare intensified, and she leaned forward, her knuckles whitening as they pressed against the polished wood. Wyatt took a small step back, then held up both hands in a placating gesture. "Before you get too worked up, hear me out."

Hannah crossed her arms. "I'm listening."

"It's not what you think," he said. "Well, it is, but it's also a fundraiser."

She blinked. "A fundraiser?"

"For the Winter Festival!" He reached beneath the counter and pulled out two large glass jars, setting them side by side on the bar. One was labeled "Team Luke" and the other "Team Carter." Each had a handwritten chart taped to the front, tracking the donations like a thermometer at a charity drive.

Hannah stared at the jars, momentarily speechless. Both were already half-full with crumpled bills and checks. There had to be at least six hundred dollars between them.

"You're telling me that half the town is betting on whether I pick Carter or Luke, and you're collecting the proceeds for the Winter Festival?"

Wyatt glanced around, then leaned in closer. "It started as a joke, honestly. A couple of the regulars were debating whether Luke or Carter would be your date for Valentine's Day. Someone suggested they put money on it, and then..." He shrugged.

"You made my love life into a punchline for the whole town."

Wyatt's expression softened. "It's not like that, Hannah. Folks are just excited, that's all. They're placing bets, sure, but they're also talking about the Festival. About the new events you're bringing in. It's the most buzz the Festival's had in years."

She dropped her forehead into her hand, partly because she couldn't decide if she wanted to laugh, cry, or strangle Wyatt on the spot.

Wyatt lowered his voice. "Look, nobody's actually betting on your heart. It's just a game. And if it means we raise enough money to pay for all of Luke and Carter's crazy ideas, where's the harm?" He set a glass of Mrs. K.'s mulled cider in front of her, as if sensing she needed it.

She took a sip of the cider, more to give herself time to collect her thoughts than because she really wanted a drink. "You didn't think to ask me before you did this?" she said, her voice low and controlled.

Wyatt leaned on the bar, as if he could

reason her into forgiveness. "Would you have said yes?"

"Of course not!" she shot back.

He nodded, as if that settled things. "That's why I didn't ask." He smiled at her with that lopsided, charming Wyatt grin. "Look. People are excited about it, Hannah. They love being part of the story. Mom says it's better than TV."

Hannah pressed her fingers to her temples. "This is a disaster."

"Or," Wyatt said, his voice dropping to a conspiratorial tone, "it's the perfect solution to your Valentine's Date dilemma. This way, you don't have to choose between them. The town decides for you."

Hannah lowered her hands, frowning. "What are you talking about?"

Wyatt's smile returned full force. "Think about it. Luke and Carter have gone all out—trying to earn your date for Valentine's Night—and eventually, you're going to have to pick one of them."

Hannah's mouth opened, then closed again. That *was* one of the things that had been keeping her up at night.

"With the betting pool," Wyatt said, "the

pressure's off. The town makes the choice, you go along with it, and everyone's happy."

Hannah took a long sip of her mulled cider, buying time to process. But before she could respond, Mrs. Peterson appeared at her elbow, a plate of buffalo wings in one hand.

"Hannah, dear! I was hoping to run into you. I just wanted to thank you and Luke and Carter for being such good sports about all this." She nodded toward the jars. "This is going to make this year's Festival the best one yet. Just yesterday, Pastor Ben was saying how impressed he is with your fundraising creativity."

Hannah's cheeks flamed. "Pastor Ben knows about this?"

"Oh, everyone does," Mrs. Peterson said cheerfully. "He hasn't placed a bet, of course—wouldn't be proper—but he did say he was looking forward to seeing how it all turns out." She patted Hannah's shoulder. "Such a wonderful addition to our community, that young man."

Hannah watched Mrs. Peterson disappear into the crowd. Ben knew about Wyatt's pool. Of course he did. In a town this size, secrets lasted about as long as ice cream in July.

"See? What did I tell you," Wyatt said. "People love it. And it's all for a good cause."

Hannah turned back to face him, torn between the desire to crawl under the bar and hide forever, and the practical realization that this pool might actually benefit the Festival. She'd been wracking her brain for weeks trying to figure out how to pay for all the extravagant additions Carter and Luke had proposed. The last thing she wanted was for the Festival to actually lose money the first year she was chair.

Now the solution had presented itself—wrapped in a package of public humiliation, but a solution, nonetheless.

Around her, the Friday crowd continued their conversations, but now that she was paying attention, Hannah could catch snippets focused on her love life:

"Luke's more dependable in the long run..."

"Have you seen the way Carter looks at her, though?"

"My money's on the vet. A man who's good with animals..."

Hannah glanced at the jars. Team Luke was currently leading by about thirty dollars, but

Team Carter appeared to have more individual contributors.

She sighed, shoulders slumping slightly as the fight drained out of her. She had started this whole dating competition to avoid embarrassment, and now she considered embracing an even more public spectacle. The irony struck her like a snowball to the face.

"So?" Wyatt prompted. "What do you say?"

Hannah took another long sip of the mulled cider and considered her options, the two jars of money on the bar a tangible reminder of what was at stake—not just her pride, but the success of the Winter Festival she'd worked so hard to plan, as well as Pastor John's faith in her ability to do this.

"Fine," she said. "I'll go along with this... this circus. But I have conditions."

Wyatt straightened, his expression shifting to attentive businessman. "Name them."

"First, no embarrassing photos or posters. No interviews about my dating life. And absolutely no social media posts on who's winning."

"Fair enough," Wyatt said.

"Second, I want regular updates on how much money we're raising."

"Absolutely. I'll text you daily totals."

"And third…" Hannah hesitated, then squared her shoulders. "I want veto power over any bets that cross the line from fun into inappropriate."

Wyatt's expression grew serious. "Hannah, I promise you—this stays respectful. Anyone gets out of line, I shut it down. You have my word." He extended his hand across the bar.

Hannah eyed his outstretched palm for a moment, then shook it firmly.

Relief washed over Wyatt's face, his posture visibly relaxing. "You won't regret this, Hannah. I promise."

"I already regret it," she said, but there was no heat in her words. "But at least the Festival will benefit."

As she passed the table of retirees near the front door, she overheard two of them—Mrs. Sandowski and Old Man Bailey—debating the finer points of Carter's charm versus Luke's dependability.

"I still say she should pick the vet," Mrs. Sandowski insisted. "They always have a way with women. All that patience."

Bailey shook his head. "Nope. The rancher's got more grit. I'm putting my money on him."

Hannah didn't break stride. She just stepped outside into the crisp February air, shaking her head at the surreal situation she'd found herself in. What had started as a simple plan to distract from one moment of impulsiveness had evolved into a town-wide event and fundraiser.

Hannah stared at the flyers crumpled at the bottom of her bag. She was supposed to give them to Mrs. K. But she'd forgotten, and there was no way she was going back inside that bar again today.

Bluestem Winter Festival. Sunday. February 10. Thanks to Wyatt's betting pool, this Festival would probably raise more money than any Festival in church memory.

And on Valentine's Day, she'd show up with whichever man the town picked for her. She'd smile and play along, just like everyone expected. Then she'd pack her bags and move to California.

Fifteen

BEN

BEN PULLED his truck into the church parking lot and cut the engine, taking a moment to survey the scene before heading inside. Vehicles filled nearly every space—Mrs. Peterson's sensible sedan, Luke's veterinary truck with its faded decal, and Carter's gleaming pickup among them.

He checked his watch: just past eight AM. Hannah had clearly told folks they didn't have to be there until at least nine. Yet the parking lot told him what he'd suspected—everyone was eager to get the Winter Festival preparations underway. He gathered his box of extra decorations from the passenger seat and headed toward the Fellowship Hall, curious about what he'd find inside.

The double doors stood propped open, and the sound of cheerful chaos spilled out into the corridor. Ben paused at the threshold, taking in the transformation already underway. What had been an empty space after Wednesday night's Bible study was now a hive of activity.

Paper snowflakes dangled from fishing line attached to the ceiling tiles, swaying gently in the current from the heating vents. Card tables lined the perimeter, some already draped in blue tablecloths, others still waiting. Minnie Frasier and her twin sister Winnie were unboxing supplies for the children's craft corner, while a cluster of teenagers stood on ladders, stringing twinkling lights along the upper walls.

And in the center of it all stood Hannah.

Even from across the room, Ben could see the rigid set of her shoulders and the way she gripped her clipboard like a shield. Her usual smile looked strained at the edges as she directed three different volunteers simultaneously. Her wild red curls had been pulled back into a ponytail that was already coming loose, stray tendrils framing her face.

She glanced down at her clipboard, checked something off with a quick, sharp motion, then looked up to scan the room again. When her gaze landed on Ben, he saw a momentary flash of something. Relief? Panic? He wasn't quite sure.

Ben set his box on a nearby table and shrugged out of his coat. He'd watched that same tension growing in Hannah over the past month—at committee meetings where Luke and Carter competed to outdo each other with increasingly elaborate festival ideas, during chance encounters at Daisy's Diner or the Rusty Spur, even last Sunday when she'd slipped into the pew next to her family, then disappeared after church before he could say hello.

Pastor John's latest phone conversation echoed in Ben's mind. "I feel terrible about leaving Hannah right before the Festival," he'd said. "She took on the chairmanship because I asked her to. I promised I'd be there every step of the way, and now..."

"Now, I'm here for her," Ben had said. And he'd meant it. The problem, of course, had been trying to figure out how to fulfill that promise without making things even more complicated.

He'd tried to be supportive without being intrusive, joining committee meetings but letting Hannah lead, offering help without hovering. It was a delicate balance—one that grew more challenging with each passing day.

Mrs. Peterson appeared at his elbow, interrupting his thoughts. "Ben! I didn't expect you so early." She handed him a mug of coffee that had materialized from somewhere. "Hannah's got everything running like a well-oiled machine. That girl is something special, isn't she?"

Ben nodded, accepting the coffee gratefully. "She certainly is." He took a sip, using the moment to gather his thoughts. "The decorations are amazing. The committee has outdone themselves."

"Oh, this is just the beginning," Mrs. Peterson said with obvious pride. "Wait until the Northern Lights display is up. Carter and Luke have been working on it all week. Speaking of which…" She nodded toward the far corner where the two men were unpacking what appeared to be elaborate lighting equipment.

Ben watched as Carter held up some sort of projector, gesturing expansively while Luke shook his head, pointing to an outlet and saying something Ben couldn't hear. Their friendly competition had intensified over the past two weeks, fueled by Wyatt's betting pool at the Rusty Spur.

Hannah approached the men, saying something that made them both laugh. For a moment, her shoulders relaxed, and Ben glimpsed the woman he'd first met at LeAnne's table on New Year's Eve—confident, bright, unguarded.

Then Lenny Beckett called her name from across the room, waving a strand of tangled lights, and the moment vanished. Her shoulders stiffened again as she hurried toward the next crisis.

Ben made his way through the room, dodging volunteers carrying boxes and strings of lights. "Good morning, everyone," he called, smiling as several people waved or nodded in his direction. "Looks like I'm late to the party."

Hannah turned at the sound of his voice. "Pastor Ben," she said, her voice sounding slightly breathless. "You didn't have to come so early."

Ben closed the distance between them,

careful to maintain what he hoped was a professional yet friendly space. "I thought I would help with setup. But it looks like you've got everything under control."

Hannah glanced around the bustling room, tucking a loose curl behind her ear. "That's what it looks like, does it?" She let out a small laugh that didn't quite reach her eyes. "I've been here since seven trying to sort out the electrical situation. Apparently, if we plug in both the Northern Lights display and the hot chocolate station, we'll blow the circuits."

She glanced down at her clipboard. "But if we move the hot chocolate station to the kitchen, people will have to walk all the way around the silent auction area to get there."

Ben set his coffee mug on a nearby table. "I have a solution for that. The church office has a heavy-duty surge protector that should fix your problem."

Relief flashed across Hannah's face. "That would be perfect. Thank you."

"I'll grab it right now."

Ben made his way out of the Fellowship Hall, navigating through clusters of volunteers. As he passed the refreshment table, he overheard Ruby Carhart's unmistakable voice.

"I've put my money on Luke," she was saying to Clayton Lesiak. "That dinner at the Rusty Spur sealed the deal for me. Did you see those photos Alyssa Downing posted? Pure romance."

Clayton shook his head. "My money's on Carter. Did you see how he showed up with those fancy lights? The man's going all out for that girl."

Ben tried to ignore their words, but they settled in his chest like a stone. The Valentine's Day pool had been amusing at first—a creative way to raise funds for the Festival. But now he found himself increasingly uncomfortable with the whole arrangement.

He retrieved the surge protector from his office and returned to find Hannah kneeling beside an electrical outlet, frowning at a tangle of cords. Her red curls had slipped further from her ponytail, and she blew a strand out of her eyes with a frustrated puff.

"Reinforcements have arrived," Ben said, holding up the heavy-duty surge protector.

"Thank you so much." She reached for the device, her fingers brushing his as she took it.

She jerked back, nearly dropping the device, then busied herself with the tangle of cords.

"What next?" he asked, rolling up his sleeves.

"We could use some help with the snowflakes," Hannah said, gesturing toward a table where a stack of white paper and scissors lay abandoned. "We need at least twenty more for the entrance hall."

"Consider it done," Ben said. He settled himself at the table, picked up the scissors, and watched as Hannah was called away, once again, by another volunteer. With a wry smile, Ben shook his head and began folding and snipping, the familiar childhood motion soothing in its repetition.

Ben kept his eye on Hannah as she moved from one crisis to another. Her exhaustion revealed itself in subtle ways—the dimming brightness of her smile, the deepening crease between her brows as the morning wore on.

When she abruptly set down her clipboard and slipped through the swinging door to the kitchen, Ben hesitated only a moment before he followed her.

The kitchen was quiet compared to the

bustling hall, the fluorescent lights humming softly overhead. Hannah stood with her back to him, leaning her hands against the stainless steel counter, her clipboard abandoned beside her. Her head was tilted forward slightly as she took slow, deep breaths.

Ben hesitated, suddenly feeling like an intruder. Perhaps she needed this moment alone. He was about to step out when she turned, her startled eyes meeting his. She straightened immediately, a smile springing to her face so quickly it might have been convincing, if he hadn't seen her a moment before.

"Pastor Ben?" she said, reaching for her clipboard. "Did you need something? Coffee? I'm just making a fresh pot."

"The only thing I need," Ben said quietly, "is to make sure you're okay."

The simple words seemed to hit Hannah like a physical force. Her shoulders slumped, and the clipboard slid from her fingers, clattering against the counter. For a moment, she just stared at him, her eyes wide and vulnerable in a way he'd never seen before.

"I'm fine," she said automatically, then winced as if recognizing the lie herself. "I mean, I'm..." She blew out a long breath that stirred the loose curls around her face. "I'm just tired. Wondering what I was thinking when I told Pastor John I would chair the Festival."

"You were thinking you wanted to help," Ben said. "To make a difference. And you have."

A silence stretched between them, broken only by the muffled sounds of activity from the Fellowship Hall and the soft hum of the refrigerator. Hannah twisted a loose curl around her finger, a habit Ben had noticed whenever she was nervous or deep in thought.

"It's just that the Festival has gotten so much bigger than what I originally planned. Carter and Luke are full of wonderful, creative ideas—the Northern Lights display, the ice sculptures, the carriage rides—but they don't think about the logistics. Who's going to set it up? Who's going to take it down? What happens if it snows?"

Hannah pushed away from the counter and began pacing the small kitchen. "And then there's this ridiculous Valentine's Day pool. Wyatt promised it would be a small, fun thing. A great way to raise money for the Festival. But now it's like the entire town has something riding on it."

She ran her hands through her hair, dislodging more curls from her ponytail. "The mayor suggested I announce my decision during tomorrow's Festival as a grand finale." Hannah's eyes widened with disbelief. "Like it's some sort of reality dating show!"

"What did you tell him?" Ben asked, curious despite himself.

"That I'd think about it." Hannah said. "I should have said no, but he looked so excited, and there were all these people standing around listening..." Her voice trailed off. "I hate disappointing people."

Hannah's gaze drifted toward the swinging doors, her expression shifting from resignation to something more complicated. "And then there's Carter and Luke themselves. They've been so supportive, so eager to help, but they're also..."

"Competitive?" Ben supplied.

"Exhausting," Hannah said, a smile appearing on her lips despite her frustration. "They're trying to outdo each other at every turn. It was funny at first, even flattering, but now..." She sighed. "Every time I turn around, one of them is there, asking what I need, offering to take over, trying to solve every problem before I can even think it through. I know they mean well, but sometimes I just want to breathe without someone hovering."

Ben nodded, careful to keep his expression neutral. If he needed confirmation that Hannah wasn't romantically interested in either man—her exasperated tone said it all.

"Have you told them how you feel?" he asked.

Hannah shook her head. "They're just trying to help. How can I complain about that?" She leaned back against the counter, suddenly looking very young and very tired. "Besides, it's just one more day. After tomorrow, the Festival will be over, the pool will be resolved, and every-thing can go back to normal."

Ben stepped closer, stopping just short of reaching for her hand. "Hannah, it's okay to tell people when you need space. Even people who care about you. Especially people who care about you."

She looked up at him, her green eyes searching his face. Her posture relaxed slightly;

her smile became more genuine. "Thank you. For listening. For not telling me I'm being ridiculous."

"You're not being ridiculous," Ben said. "You're being human."

The kitchen door swung open with such force that it banged against the wall, making both Ben and Hannah jump. Carter strode in first, his broad shoulders filling the doorway, with Luke only a half-step behind him.

"There you are!" Carter said, his voice a touch too loud for the small kitchen. "We've been looking everywhere for you."

"Hannah, we need your help with the volunteer assignments," Luke said. "There's some confusion about the craft station rotation."

Hannah straightened, her moment of vulnerability evaporating like morning mist. "What's the problem?" she asked, slipping effortlessly back into her role as festival chair.

Carter moved to her side, creating a subtle barrier between Hannah and Ben. "Minnie and Winnie both want the morning shift, but we need someone experienced for the afternoon when it's busiest."

"That's not really a problem," Hannah said,

frowning slightly. "Minnie always takes morning shifts because of her arthritis. We discussed this at the last meeting."

"Right, but..." Luke said, as if searching for something to say. "There's also an issue with the silent auction. Ruby wants to know if we're doing bid sheets or auction paddles."

Ben watched as Hannah's eyes narrowed almost imperceptibly. These weren't urgent issues requiring an immediate consultation in the kitchen. These were routine questions any committee member could have handled, or at the very least, waited until Hannah returned to the hall.

"Bid sheets," Hannah said firmly. "Just like we agreed last week." She glanced back at Ben with an apologetic smile. "I should go sort this out. Thanks for the pep talk."

As Hannah moved toward the door, Carter leaned down to whisper something in her ear that made her shake her head with a reluctant smile, while Luke rested his hand briefly at the small of her back, guiding her through the doorway.

The coffee finished brewing, and Ben filled a large carafe, then arranged everything neatly on the tray. He took a deep breath, squared his shoulders, and pushed through the door back into the Fellowship Hall.

He set the coffee tray on the refreshment table and busied himself with arranging napkins and stirrers in neat rows. From this vantage point, he could observe the room without being obvious about it. Hannah once again moved from station to station, her professional demeanor firmly back in place, but there was a new lightness in her step that hadn't been there earlier. Her conversation with him seemed to have helped, at least a little.

Across the room, a shaft of winter sunlight streamed through the stained glass windows, casting patterns of blue and purple across the busy hall. Hannah stepped into the light, her red hair glowing with blue and gold highlights, and Ben felt his breath catch.

As he stood there, mesmerized, Hannah glanced up from across the room and smiled at him. Ben smiled back, wondering what it would be like to see that smile directed at him every morning. To have those green eyes meet his across a breakfast table rather than a church hall filled with volunteers.

He stilled his hands, letting the thought settle before carefully setting it aside. Not now, not yet. The timing wasn't right for either of them. But as Hannah's laugh carried across the room, warming something deep in his chest, Ben knew with quiet certainty: Hannah Mitchell was someone worth waiting for. And for now, that knowledge was enough.

Sixteen

BEN

THE SILENCE of the church greeted Ben as he slipped through the side door. The sanctuary stretched before him, a silent sea of empty pews bathed in the soft glow of dawn, filtered through stained glass windows. Ben had grown to love this moment—this sacred pause before the day began in earnest, when he could gather his thoughts and commune with God without inter-ruption.

Usually, it calmed him. Today, though, the silence felt heavier somehow, more significant, as if the pews themselves were waiting with particular expectation for the words that he would speak in just a few hours.

Ben climbed the steps to the pulpit and laid out his notes, smoothing the pages with his palm. He set his travel mug on the small table beside the pulpit and checked his watch: 7:37 AM. In a few short hours, worshippers would fill this sanctuary, and immediately after, the church grounds would transform into the Winter Festival. Hannah's Festival. But for now, the church was his alone.

Ben took a deep breath. He'd chosen 1 Corinthians 13—the love chapter—for today's message. It seemed fitting, with Valentine's Day approaching. His finger traced the verse numbers: 4 through 7. Words he'd read hundreds of times, words he'd studied in seminary, words he'd shared with couples during premarital counseling.

Words that suddenly felt painfully personal.

Ben adjusted the microphone more out of habit than necessity. The sanctuary was empty; there was no one to hear him practice except God. He cleared his throat and spoke, the sound of his own voice echoing against the vaulted ceiling.

"Love is patient, love is kind."

The words sounded bigger in the empty sanctuary. He thought of his grandparents, how they'd lived out those words every day through sixty years of marriage. That was the love he'd always pictured for himself: unwavering, gentle, strong.

"It does not envy, it does not boast, it is not proud."

He kept going, his voice gaining power as he moved through the lines.

"It does not dishonor others. It is not self-seeking. It is not easily angered, it keeps no record of wrongs."

His voice caught. Hannah's face appeared in his mind, unbidden. Hannah with her wild red curls and those luminous, searching eyes. Hannah, who blushed so fiercely when embarrassed. Hannah, who despite being surrounded by friends, sometimes seemed so achingly alone.

Hannah, who filled his thoughts more and more each day.

Ben ran a hand through his hair. Could he preach about love while pretending not to feel it himself? It seemed wrong—a lie, or close to it. But what was the alternative? To admit to these feelings out loud would only tangle things further.

"Love does not delight in evil but rejoices with the truth."

Truth. The word hung in the air. What was his truth? That Hannah intrigued him? Yes. That her spark and impulsiveness countered his steadiness in ways that felt surprisingly right? Absolutely. That as the interim pastor, trying to build trust with this congregation, the timing couldn't be worse? No denying that.

"It always protects, always trusts, always hopes, always perseveres."

He thought of the moment in the kitchen yesterday: Hannah, letting down her guard just enough to confess her fatigue and frustration. The connection that had sparked between them, unguarded and real, before Carter and Luke had swept in.

Carter and Luke. It was becoming more and more obvious that it wasn't romance that bound the three of them—it was friendship. Genuine, deep-rooted friendship. The kind that would make two grown men stage an increasingly ridiculous dating competition just to protect their friend from — what exactly? Small-town gossip? One small impulsive kiss on a night filled with kisses?

It was a different kind of love than what Ben felt stirring in his own heart, but no less real. Their friendship had shifted something in his perspective. Not just about Hannah, but about what love truly meant.

Love was so complicated. And it came in so many forms. The love between friends. The love between family members. The love between a pastor and his congregation. And sometimes, the love that blossoms and grows between two specific people.

Ben dropped his head. "Lord," he whispered, "give me wisdom. Show me the path forward—whether that means waiting, or speaking, or simply serving as I've been called to do."

The prayer was simple, honest. No flowery language, no theological complexity. Just the raw need of a man seeking guidance.

He touched the pages of his typed sermon gently, running his finger along the underlined passage: "Love never fails."

Whatever happened—with Hannah, with the church, with his life going forward—that truth remained. Love, in its purest form, never failed. It might not follow the path expected or arrive as anticipated, but it remained steadfast. Like his faith. Like his calling.

When the congregation gathered in a few hours, he would speak about love with honesty and conviction. He would meet Hannah's eyes if she looked his way, without expectation or pressure. He would guide his flock with the integrity they deserved, keeping his personal feelings in check without denying their existence.

And later, when the Winter Festival transformed the church grounds into a celebration of community and connection, he would take part fully, helping where needed, observing the fruits of Hannah's hard work with genuine appreciation.

The timing wasn't right yet for any type of declaration. He felt that truth in his bones. But "yet" was a powerful word, full of possibility. For now, he would focus on being the pastor Bluestem needed. The rest would unfold as it was meant to, in its own time.

Ben straightened his shoulders and checked his watch again. Almost 8:30. Soon Mrs. Peterson would arrive to prepare the bulletin, and the day would begin in earnest. He took a sip of his now-lukewarm coffee and turned to the closing lines of his sermon.

"These three remain: faith, hope and love. But the greatest of these is love."

Seventeen

HANNAH

The Winter Festival had always been a highlight of the year for Hannah. Part county fair, part church potluck, smack dab in the middle of the longest short month of the year—February.

Even when Hannah was a kid, she'd loved the way the church was transformed overnight—how the stained-glass windows spilled colored light onto tables brimming with baked goods and silent auction baskets, how the fellowship hall echoed with the laughter of friends and neighbors who'd known each other most of their lives.

This year, though, it was different. This year, she was the chair. The woman in charge. And she wasn't arriving alone or with her family. Instead, Carter and Luke had insisted that both of them should have the honor of escorting her to the Festival—so it wouldn't look like she'd already made her choice. She'd relented—on the strict condition that they tone down their constant one-upmanship, at least for today.

So here she was, sandwiched between Carter and Luke like a reluctant celebrity with her security detail.

Inside, the fellowship hall buzzed with last-minute activity. The room had been transformed: tables draped in snowflake-patterned cloths, silver garlands twined around every doorframe, and twinkling lights strung from the tiles overhead. The air smelled like cinnamon rolls and chili, coffee and cocoa.

Alyssa waved from behind the camera she'd set up near the entrance. "Smile, you three!" She snapped a photo as Carter slung an arm around Hannah's shoulders and Luke held up a peace sign.

"Do you ever take a break?" Hannah asked, ducking out from under Carter's arm.

"Look who's talking!" Alyssa said. "The

woman who's been working on this thing night and day for the past four months."

Before she could muster a comeback, Mrs. K. appeared with a tray of donuts, shoving one into Hannah's hand. "Eat," she ordered. "No one likes a hangry chairwoman." Then, softer, "You're doing great, kiddo. Don't let these two clowns get to you."

Hannah nibbled at her donut, grateful for the sugar rush. She scanned the room, taking in the scene: the Frasier twins setting up the cake walk, Ruby Carhart organizing the ticket table, and a dozen volunteers wrangling the silent auction items onto the stage.

At the far end of the hall, Ben stood with a group of elderly church members, guiding them through the setup for the raffle. He wore a blue wool sweater, its sleeves pushed up. Their eyes met for a moment, and Ben's face lit up with a smile.

That smile landed like a spark, igniting a warmth that spread through her chest and chased away some of the morning's chill. She quickly dropped her gaze, and focused on the organized chaos around her. This was her Festival. Her responsibility. This had to be her focus for today.

As the clock struck one, the doors to the Festival officially opened. Ben took the stage, microphone in hand. "Good morning, everyone! I'm Pastor Ben Landry, and I want to thank you all for coming out to support Bluestem Community Church's Winter Festival."

"We've got a full day ahead: games, contests, chili cook-off, and of course, the silent auction. But first, a round of applause for the person who made this all possible—our Festival Chair, Hannah Mitchell."

The applause was deafening. Carter wolf-whistled, Luke clapped so hard his hands turned red, and Mrs. K. beamed from the kitchen door. Hannah ducked her head, trying to hide the blush that crept up her neck.

"You've outdone yourself, Mitchell," Carter said, his breath warm against her ear as he leaned close. "This place looks even better than it did yesterday."

Luke nodded his agreement. "The Northern Lights theme really makes a difference. And I think there's already a line forming for the portrait booth."

"The carriage rides are starting in fifteen minutes," Carter said, checking his watch. "And I have secured us the very first ride." He gave her a wink. "Being friends with the guy who brought the carriage has its perks."

Hannah glanced out the window where children were already creating snow angels on the church lawn, their colorful winter coats bright against the snow. Parents snapped photos and chatted with each other as their children played.

"Go ahead," Luke said, nudging her toward the door. "I'll man your post at the welcome table for a bit."

Hannah hesitated, a flutter of guilt rising in her chest. She'd barely had time to check that everything was running smoothly. "I should really make sure the cocoa station is—"

"You know Mrs. K. is in charge of that station. Trust me, no one's going thirsty on her watch."

Carter placed a hand at the small of her back, steering her gently toward the coat rack. "Besides, how can you say no to a ride in a carriage? This is your Festival, Hannah. You should get to enjoy at least some of it."

Outside, the air was crisp and clean, the kind

of cold that nipped at cheeks and turned noses pink. Carter led her around the side of the church where two magnificent Belgians stamped their hooves, their breath forming clouds in the frosty air as they waited, harnessed to an antique carriage.

"Carter Manchester, this is not what I expected when you said 'carriage rides,'" Hannah said, unable to hide her delight. "I thought it would be one of those little one-horse deals, not... this." She gestured at the beautiful six-seater carriage, which gleamed with polished wood and red velvet seat cushions.

Carter grinned, clearly pleased with her reaction. "Only the best for the chairwoman of the Winter Festival." He held out his hand to help her up, then climbed in beside her, tucking a thick blanket over their laps.

The driver—a weathered man in a sheepskin coat—clicked his tongue, and the horses lurched forward, bells jingling from their harnesses.

The carriage rolled down Main Street, bells jingling in time with the horses' steps. The town looked magical: every storefront window frosted with snow, the trees strung with lights, the sun shining in a perfect blue sky.

Luke gestured to the crowd lining the route. "Looks like you're the grand marshal of Bluestem, Hannah."

She laughed, waving at the clusters of kids who cheered as the carriage passed by. For a few minutes, she allowed herself to forget about the New Year's kiss and the Valentine's Day pool and pretend romances. She was simply Hannah Mitchell, enjoying a perfect winter afternoon with one of her favorite people.

"See? Worth it?" Carter asked, nudging her with his elbow.

Hannah nodded, watching the children point and wave as they passed. "It really is. Thank you."

"No problem," Carter said. "I just made a few phone calls."

"Not just for the carriage," Hannah said. "For... everything. The picnics and the flowers and the silly competition with Luke. I know you've both been going overboard to help me."

Carter's expression softened. "That's what friends do, Hannah. Besides, Luke and I are having a blast. It's not every day we get to play knights in shining armor." He leaned back against the seat cushions, his posture relaxed.

"And don't tell him I said this, but Luke's been a worthy opponent."

The horses completed their circuit, returning Hannah and Carter to the church entrance just as a small crowd gathered for the next ride. Hannah stepped down, her cheeks flushed from the cold and the surprising rush of joy the ride had given her. If this wonderful start was any indication, the rest of this day was going to be truly magical.

Eighteen

BEN STOOD at the edge of the fellowship hall, a cup of coffee warming his hands. Kids zigzagged between tables covered in the snowflake tablecloths, their laughter ringing out over the friendly chatter of the adults.

He watched as Hannah came through the front door, returning from her carriage ride. Her cheeks were flushed pink from the cold, her smile wider and more genuine than he'd seen since New Year's Eve. Carter followed close behind her, his usual confident swagger punctuated by an easy laugh as he retold some story that had Hannah shaking her head, snowflakes still clinging to her wild red curls.

"Quite a turnout, isn't it?" Lenny Beckett appeared at Ben's side. "Hannah's done a remarkable job. I don't think I've ever seen this many people at the Winter Festival."

"She certainly has," Ben agreed, his gaze still following Hannah as she moved through the crowd. "Everything looks wonderful."

Lenny nodded, his eyes shining as he followed Ben's line of sight. "She's special, that one. Always has been." He patted Ben's arm and hustled away before he could respond.

Ben shifted his weight from one foot to the other, wondering if he should be more careful about how openly he watched Hannah. But then again, everyone was watching her today. She was the chairwoman, after all, and it was her festival.

Across the room, Luke approached Hannah, his hands tucked behind his back. From the way Hannah's eyebrows rose, Ben could tell she was responding to whatever Luke was hiding. With a flourish, Luke revealed an oversized plush snowman, its felt carrot nose slightly askew, black button eyes gleaming under the hall lights.

Hannah's face lit up with such genuine

delight that Ben found himself smiling in response. She took the snowman, hugging it to her chest while saying something that made Luke laugh. Luke ran a hand through his hair, the gesture modest, and pointed toward the raffle table. Hannah glanced in that direction, then back at Luke, her smile softening into something grateful and affectionate.

Ben looked away. He tightened his grip on his coffee cup, the warmth no longer comforting. He had no right to the unexpected jealousy that pricked at his chest. He'd been in Bluestem barely six weeks; Luke and Carter had known Hannah for years.

Besides, he reminded himself, Hannah deserved a day of simple joy, of being celebrated by people who cared about her.

Ben set his empty cup on a nearby table and made his way toward the silent auction. Brightly wrapped baskets filled one corner of the fellowship hall—everything from homemade quilts to fishing equipment to a weekend stay at the Whitemore Hotel. He examined each item, noting the generous donations from local businesses and church members alike.

"See anything you like, Pastor?"

Ben turned to find Hannah standing beside him. "I'm still deciding," Ben said, his throat suddenly dry. The real answer was right on the tip of his tongue—what he wanted most was standing right in front of him with snowflakes melting in her hair and a ridiculous plush snowman clasped in her arms.

Hannah's eyes sparkled. "Don't wait too long. All the good stuff will be gone."

"I'll keep that in mind," Ben said, trying to match her light tone.

She glanced at her watch. "I should get back. We're starting the children's games soon, and I promised Mrs. Peterson I'd help judge the snowman-building contest."

Ben watched her go, his hands finding their way into his pockets. Lenny Beckett's words echoed in his mind: She's special, that one. Always has been.

"Pastor Ben!" Mrs. Peterson's voice cut through his thoughts. She waved from the side door that led to the church lawn, her breath visible in the cold air. "We're starting the snowman-building contest. Come join us!"

Ben nodded and made his way outside,

pausing to grab his coat from the rack by the door. The crisp February air bit at his cheeks as he stepped onto the church lawn, already trampled by dozens of footprints. A sizeable crowd had gathered in a loose circle, their faces bright with anticipation despite the cold.

"Aren't those two men wonderful?" Mrs. Peterson said, pointing to Luke and Carter, standing in the yard, surrounded by a cluster of elementary-aged children. "They've both agreed to take part in the snowman-building contest. The kids are thrilled!"

Ben tried hard to stifle his exasperation. Those two had even found a way to turn a children's activity into a competition, and managed to charm his church secretary while they did it.

Mrs. Peterson said "Go" and the race was on. Carter helped his team roll a massive snowball for the base, while Luke instructed his young teammates on the proper technique for packing snow.

Ben watched from the church steps, grinning despite himself, as both men became ten years old again, tunnel-visioned and determined. Luke's team was building a traditional snowman, complete with stick arms, a carrot nose, and a winter scarf. Carter's team had opted for a snow-woman, with a skirt made of packed snow and pine branches for hair.

"Time's almost up!" Mrs. Peterson called. "Ten more minutes!"

Both teams worked frantically, their young helpers shrieking with laughter as they patted and shaped their creations. Carter's team was falling behind, their snow-woman still missing a face and arms. Luke's team had nearly finished, their snowman impressively detailed.

"Need to step up your game, Manchester," Luke called, packing more snow onto their creation's head. "Looks like your snowman's going to be the ugly duckling of the Festival."

Carter straightened, his competitive streak visibly ignited. "Oh yeah?" He scooped up a handful of snow, packed it into a loose ball, and lobbed it at Luke's shoulder.

Luke froze, then slowly turned, a dangerous grin spreading across his face. "Did you just—"

"What are you going to do about it, Merriwether?" Carter asked, already packing another snowball.

Luke's response was swift and accurate, a perfectly formed snowball catching Carter square in the chest. The children shrieked with laughter, and within seconds, the snowman-building competition had dissolved into an all-out snowball fight. The children gathered behind their team leaders, and the church lawn was a battlefield of flying snow. Carter took refuge behind their half-built snow woman, while Luke commandeered a pile of pre-made snowballs that some of the older kids had created earlier.

Ben found himself caught between amusement and concern. The snowballs flew thick and fast now, most of them soft and harmless. But the competitive energy between Carter and Luke hadn't dissipated—if anything, it had intensified.

Ben saw Carter pack a snowball with particular care, a competitive glint in his eyes.

"Carter, don't—" Hannah called, but it was too late.

Carter launched the snowball with full force, aiming for Luke, who ducked at the last second. The icy projectile sailed over Luke's head and continued its arc directly toward the church.

Time seemed to slow as Ben watched the snowball strike a small stained glass window—

one of several that lined the fellowship hall. For a moment, nothing happened.

Then they heard it; the distinctive crack of breaking glass, and the window shattered, sending a spray of colored glass into the fellowship hall.

Even from where he stood, Ben could see the damage—a jagged hole in the center of the window, colorful shards scattered across the snow and sidewalk beneath. The window had depicted Jesus in a field, surrounded by sheep, and now his face was gone, leaving only an empty space with sharp, fractured edges.

The children froze, snowballs clutched in mittened hands. Parents' mouths hung open in mid-cheer. Carter stood stock-still, his face drained of color. Luke straightened slowly, the snowball in his hand falling forgotten to the ground. Everyone seemed to be holding their breath, waiting for someone—anyone—to react first.

Ben instinctively stepped forward, preparing to take charge of the situation as the pastor. But then his gaze fell on Hannah, and what he saw made him pause. Her face had gone still, a complicated mixture of emotions washing across her features—shock, dismay, and something deeper that looked almost like resignation.

She stood motionless for a heartbeat, then she squared her shoulders and moved purposefully toward the inside of the fellowship hall.

Ben followed, wanting to help, but not sure what to do. There was something both vulnerable and commanding in her posture as she climbed the stage steps and adjusted the microphone.

Hannah's gaze swept over the assembled faces. "Attention everyone," she said, her voice cracking. "There's been an accident. I'm afraid we need to end the Festival early today because of safety concerns with the broken glass." She paused, allowing the information to sink in. "I want to thank everyone for coming out to support our church. We hope to see you next year."

For a second, nobody moved. Then, as if released from a spell, everyone began to talk and move at the same time.

Hannah stepped away from the stage and moved to the window, where Clayton Lesiak was already examining the damage. Ben headed in their direction.

"We're going to have to cover up this hole," Clayton was saying. "I've got some plywood in my truck. And a tarp. That will do for now."

Hannah nodded. "Perfect. Thank you, Clayton." She turned, nearly colliding with Ben. "Pastor Ben. I was just coming to find you."

Up close, he could see the strain around her eyes that her composed voice didn't reveal. The freckles across her nose stood out starkly against her pale skin, and a single curl had escaped her ponytail, dangling beside her left ear.

"What would you like me to do?" he asked.

"Could you help people gather their things and get on their way? The sooner we can get the hall cleared, the better." She glanced back at the broken window, where a sharp gust of wind was now scattering snowflakes through the jagged hole.

Ben nodded, fighting the urge to reach out and tuck that wayward curl behind her ear. "I'll handle the evacuation," he said, keeping his voice steady to match hers. "You focus on the clean up."

"Thank you," she said, her voice steadier now. Their eyes met briefly, and in that moment, Ben saw not just the exhaustion, but a flicker of something more vulnerable—a momentary crack in her carefully maintained composure.

The next two hours passed in a blur of practical tasks. Ben helped carry boxes to storage, assisted with folding the last of the tablecloths, and thanked the remaining volunteers as they departed. All the while, he kept Hannah in his peripheral vision, noting how her movements grew increasingly mechanical, her responses more clipped.

She was holding herself together with visible effort now. The calm authority that had impressed him earlier had hardened into something more brittle—a shell that seemed dangerously close to cracking.

The fellowship hall was mostly empty now, except for Alyssa, Riley, Carter, and Luke, huddled at a table in the back of the room, and Hannah, standing alone in the center of the room. She was surveying the space, her gaze moving from the now-bare walls to the folded tables to the entrance where, only hours earlier, festival-goers had crowded with excitement.

Ben approached her slowly, careful not to startle her. "Hannah, can I drive you home? You've been on your feet all day."

She turned toward him, her eyes meeting his for a moment before sliding away. "No, thank you, Ben. I have my car here." Her gaze darted around the room, not landing on any of them. "But you're right. I am tired. I think I should probably go home now."

Luke and Carter approached them, their expressions serious. "Hannah, we—" Carter began.

But Hannah turned her back on them as she gathered up her coat and purse. "Not now, Guys. I can't talk to you now." The words came out in a rush, her movements growing increasingly jerky as she fumbled with her coat buttons.

"Hannah, wait," Luke said, reaching out but stopping short of actually touching her. "We're so sorry about the window. Carter and I will cover all of the costs. And any other damages. The whole thing was just—"

"Just what?" she asked. "A mistake? An accident?"

It was at that exact moment that her carefully maintained composure shattered, like the glass of that stained glass window. Her eyes filled with tears, her breath hitched, and without another word, she turned and fled toward the exit.

"Hannah!" Alyssa called, moving to follow her.

Hannah pushed through the exit and out into the parking lot, racing toward her car as she fumbled for her keys.

"Hannah, wait!" Ben called, Carter and Luke's voices echoing his own. By the time they reached the parking lot, Hannah was already starting her car. They stood in a loose semicircle —Ben, Alyssa, Riley, Carter, and Luke— watching helplessly as Hannah's car backed out of its space and pulled away, tires spinning slightly on the slick parking lot surface.

"Maybe I should go after her," Alyssa said, turning to Riley for confirmation.

"Maybe not," Ben said. "I think she needs a little time to herself. To process what happened today on her own."

Reluctantly, Alyssa agreed.

As the rest of the group gathered their things and left, Ben lingered in the parking lot. He stood in the space where Hannah's car had been, snow beginning to fill in the tire tracks she'd left behind. The church was dark now except for a single security light.

The wind picked up, carrying a few snowflakes that stung his cheeks. Ben pulled his collar higher and thought of Hannah, driving home alone, upset and exhausted. The urge to ignore his own advice and follow her, to make sure she was all right, pressed against his ribs like a physical ache.

He climbed in and started the engine, but instead of heading straight back to the Hotel, found himself taking the long route home—the one that led past Hannah's cottage. He wasn't planning to stop or intrude. He just needed to know she'd made it safely home, needed that small reassurance before he could rest tonight.

As he drove slowly past her place, he saw her porch light on and her car in the driveway. Through the front window, a soft light glowed. She was home.

But that wasn't all that he saw. A caravan of three pickup trucks cruised the street ahead of him. Riley and Alyssa, Carter, and Luke. Ben smiled ruefully. It seemed they'd all ignored his advice.

Ben breathed a sigh of relief and headed for

the Whitemore. Whatever words of comfort he might have to offer could wait until she was ready to hear them. For now, all he could do was pray that she would find some measure of peace tonight, and that tomorrow would bring healing for both the broken window and Hannah's wounded spirit.

Nineteen

HANNAH

HANNAH REACHED her cottage just as darkness settled across Bluestem, the streetlights flickering on one by one. She let herself in, locked the door, and left her boots and coat in a heap on the mat. For a long time, she just stood in the entryway, staring at nothing, numb all the way through.

She was exhausted, but the shame and anger and heartbreak made her restless. She made it as far as her bed before the tears came. Not the pretty, cinematic kind, but the ugly, hiccupping kind that made her nose run and her mascara smudge.

She cried for the broken window, for the ruined Festival, for every stupid choice she'd made since New Year's Eve. She cried until her eyes burned and her throat ached, until the only sound left was her own ragged breathing.

She must have fallen asleep at some point, because when she woke, the room was dim and the clock on her phone said 9:02. Luke's plush snowman sat in the corner, staring at her with its stupid, lopsided smile.

She rolled over and reached for her phone, the screen lighting up with a stack of missed messages and notifications. She wiped her face with the sleeve of her sweater and scrolled through the texts.

Two texts and two missed calls from Alyssa. Multiple text messages from Luke and Carter. Three texts from Ben. Two texts from her mom, and one from her brother, Josh.

She opened Ben's messages first, somehow knowing they would be the easiest to bear.

> I wanted to check in and make sure you're all right.

> Please don't blame yourself for what happened. Accidents happen at community events.

I'm here if you need to talk.
Anytime.

Hannah read that last one over and over, her thumb hovering above the reply button. She wanted to say something—anything—but every word she thought of sounded hollow or pathetic. How do you apologize to someone you barely know for turning their first month in a new town into a nightmare?

She read Carter's texts next, each one more desperate than the last.

Hannah, I am SO sorry. I don't even know what to say.

Please let me know you're okay.

I know you're mad and you have every right to be. But please just tell me you're okay.

Luke's messages followed a similar pattern, moving from apology to worry to outright panic.

Hannah, we messed up. Big time. I'm so sorry.

> Carter and I are going to fix this.
> The window, everything.

> I'm really worried about you.
> Please, just text back so I know
> you're alive.

Alyssa's were different in tone but equally concerned.

> I'm here if you need to talk. Or if
> you need ice cream and
> someone to help you plot
> revenge.

> Seriously, Hannah. I'm worried.
> Text me back.

She scrolled through her family's messages, her chest tightening with a fresh wave of embarrassment.

From her mom:

> Sweetheart, call me when you
> can. Are you all right?

A second text, sent a few minutes later:

> Let us know if you want to come
> over. I'll make your favorite:
> White Chicken Chili.

From Josh, her younger brother:

> Saw the snowball fight.
> Manchester's got a nasty
> curveball, huh? Hang in there,
> Sis. If you need a distraction, I'm
> up for frozen pizza and a bad
> movie.

Hannah dropped the phone onto her night-stand and leaned her head back against the mattress, staring at the ceiling. What a mess. What an absolute disaster of a day. She'd spent months planning that festival, countless hours organizing volunteers and coordinating events. And for what? For it to end with broken glass and public humiliation.

The worst part wasn't even the window. It was knowing that half the town had witnessed her festival implode, the same half that had been placing bets on her love life for two weeks. By tomorrow, everyone in the county would have heard about this, about how the Community Church's big Winter Festival ended with a stained glass window broken into a million pieces.

She closed her eyes, remembering the sickening sound of glass shattering, the horrified gasps from the crowd. The looks of genuine remorse on Luke and Carter's faces. They hadn't meant for things to go so wrong—she knew that. What had started as a silly plan to distract the town from her New Year's Eve kiss had spiraled completely out of control.

And yet, wasn't that exactly what always happened with her? Acting without thinking. Leaping before she looked. Making impulsive decisions that came back to haunt her. First kissing Ben, then agreeing to this charade with Luke and Carter, then allowing Wyatt's betting pool to continue. At every turn, she'd chosen the path that seemed easiest in the moment, only to find herself deeper in the mess.

Hannah reached for a tissue and wiped her eyes. The room was fully dark now, but she made no move to turn on a light. The darkness felt appropriate somehow, matching her mood.

Her phone lit up again. Another text from Carter:

> Please, Hannah. Just let us
> know you're okay.

She picked up the phone, staring at the message. The anger and frustration that had propelled her out of the church and all the way home had faded, leaving behind a bone-deep exhaustion and a surprising clarity. This had to end. All of it. The pretend dating, the Valentine's Day pool, the gossip, the evasion. No more hiding behind Luke and Carter to avoid facing the consequences of that impulsive New Year's Eve kiss.

Hannah straightened her shoulders and unlocked her phone. Instead of replying to any of the individual messages, she started a new group text to Luke and Carter, and added Wyatt's name.

> Meet me at the Rusty Spur
> tomorrow morning at nine. We
> need to talk.

She hit send before she could second-guess herself, then added:

And yes, I know the broken
window wasn't intentional. But
this whole thing has gone way
too far.

She set her phone down and switched on her bedside lamp, the warm light pushing back the shadows. She forced herself out of bed and shuffled down to the kitchen. As she fixed herself a cup of cocoa, Hannah felt a strange sense of calm settle over her. She couldn't control what the town would say about today's disaster, but she could control what she did about the disaster.

Her phone buzzed three times in rapid succession. Three replies, almost simultaneously.

CARTER

We'll be there. And Hannah... I
really am sorry.

LUKE

Nine sharp. Thank you for giving
us a chance to make this right.

WYATT

See you all tomorrow morning.
Door will be open. Coffee will be
ready.

Hannah stared at the replies, feeling a small measure of relief they had all responded so quickly. But she wasn't done yet.

She opened a new message to Alyssa, typing quickly before she lost her nerve.

> I'm okay. Just needed some time by myself. Thank you for checking on me. Can we talk tomorrow after I meet with the guys?

She hit send, then started typing to her mom.

> Hi Mom. I'm fine, just embarrassed about how the Festival ended. Rain check on the soup? I need to sort some things out first, but I'll call you tomorrow.

Finally, she typed a message to Josh, managing a small smile despite everything.

> Your sister survived another public humiliation. Thanks for asking. Frozen pizza and a bad movie sound perfect, but maybe next weekend? I have some cleanup to do first. Literally and figuratively.

She sent the messages and set her phone on her nightstand. Tomorrow, she would put an end to this ridiculous competition. She would tackle the town's gossip head-on. She would clean up the mess she'd helped create.

And maybe, just maybe, she'd finally have the courage to face the last person on her list—the one whose texts she'd read first, but hadn't yet found the courage to answer.

Twenty

HANNAH

THROUGH THE FROSTED glass of the Rusty Spur's window, Hannah saw their silhouettes: Luke, Carter, and Wyatt. She almost turned back, her boots shifting in the snow, but forced her feet to stay planted on the sidewalk. Taking a breath that misted in front of her face, she reached for the door.

The bell above her head chimed its familiar greeting as the door swung open. It was an hour before the bar officially opened, so it was eerily empty. Three heads turned in her direction. Carter pushed halfway out of his chair, his usual swagger replaced by something raw and uncertain. Luke stared at her, his jaw working silently. Wyatt stood behind the polished bar, dishtowel forgotten in his hands, face carefully neutral.

"Hannah," Carter said, barely above a whisper. He took a half-step toward her, then seemed to catch himself, stopping beside the table with one hand gripping the back of his chair. "Thanks for coming."

She nodded, feeling the tension pull at the muscles in her neck. She shrugged off her coat, the wool heavy with melted snow, and draped it over an empty chair. The wooden legs scraped against the worn floorboards as she pulled it out, the sound unnaturally loud in the quiet space. She sat with her back straight and folded her hands on the scarred tabletop, her fingers interlaced to keep them steady.

"Can I get you anything?" Wyatt's voice carried across the room as he held up a clean mug. "Coffee? Tea?"

"Just water, please," Hannah said.

Wyatt filled a glass from a pitcher of ice water and walked it over to the table. He set it down in front of her, his eyes meeting hers briefly with something that might have been encouragement, or maybe apology. The silence settled over them like a heavy blanket. Luke cleared his throat, the sound rough in the stillness. Carter's fingers began a nervous rhythm against the wooden table, their tap-tap-tap the only movement in the room.

Hannah wrapped her icy fingers around the glass and instantly regretted her choice of drink. She set the ice-cold glass down without taking a sip and looked at each of them in turn.

Luke spoke first, his brown eyes clouded with genuine regret. "Hannah, before you say anything, I just... we're so sorry. For everything."

"The snowball fight, the window, the Festival ending early." Carter leaned forward on his elbows, his words tumbling out in a rush. "We got completely carried away. This whole dating competition... it was supposed to be fun. It was never supposed to hurt you. Or the church."

Hannah met their gaze steadily, letting the weight of their apology settle between them. "The Winter Festival is over," she said, her voice gaining strength with each word. "And that means the Valentine's Day contest is officially over, too. Which means no winner—of the pool or the date."

Luke and Carter exchanged a look that spoke of shared guilt and mutual understanding.

"We know," Luke said.

Carter nodded, some of his natural energy returning. "I talked with Pastor Ben this morning before I came over here. There's a specialist in Omaha who restores stained glass. Ben said he can fix it so it will be as good as new by Easter."

Hannah felt a small flutter of relief, though she kept her expression neutral.

"And I'm covering the entire cost," Carter said, his tone brooking no argument.

"We're both covering it," Luke corrected, shooting Carter a look that was part annoyance, part affection. "We messed up together, we'll fix it together."

"That's… good. Thank you." She let out a sigh. "But it doesn't change the fact that this whole thing went way too far." Her eyes locked onto Wyatt across the room. "The pool ends today. No more money, no more updates, no more speculation about my love life."

Wyatt nodded. "Already done, Hannah. I sent a message out this morning. I gave folks the option to take their money back or donate it to the church for the Winter Festival. Most folks are choosing to donate."

Wyatt reached under the counter and pulled out the two large glass jars. Wadded bills and small, sealed envelopes filled each of them—each envelope bearing someone's name and their donation. "We raised nine hundred and thirty-five dollars total. It'll help cover the cost of shutting the Festival down early."

Hannah felt a flutter of surprise and mortification. Nine hundred dollars. All that money, all that attention focused on her romantic life, and for what? A shattered window and a festival that would go down in Bluestem history for all the wrong reasons.

For a long moment, the four of them sat in the quiet bar, the weight of the past six weeks settling upon them. Hannah looked from Luke's earnest, regretful face to Carter's unusually subdued expression, and finally to Wyatt and the two jars filled with money, sitting on the bar like some bizarre trophies. All this chaos, all this hurt, because she'd been too afraid to face the consequences of one impulsive kiss under the mistletoe.

"I should have shut this down weeks ago,"

she said, the confession coming easier than she'd expected. "I was so embarrassed about kissing Ben that I turned my life into some kind of reality competition."

"We didn't help," Luke said, a wry smile tugging at the corner of his mouth. "If anything, we made it a thousand times worse."

"But it was fun, wasn't it?" Carter asked, and Hannah caught a bit of the old Manchester mischief in his voice. "At least, some of it? Before the snowball fight."

Despite herself, Hannah felt a smile tug at the corner of her lips. "Some of it was fun," she said. "The carriage ride. The picnic. That amazing dinner here."

Her smile faded as she thought about what came next. She pushed back her chair and stood, gathering her purse and coat. "I need to go talk to Ben."

"Want company?" Luke asked, his tone gentle. "Moral support?"

Hannah shook her head as she slipped on her coat. "This is something I need to do myself." She looked at them—all three of them—these men who had helped create this disastrous, complicated, beautiful mess. "Thank you. All of you. For everything you did to help me. Even if it didn't exactly turn out the way we planned."

"Let us know how it goes," Wyatt said, his eyes holding hers with genuine concern.

Hannah nodded. "I will."

As she stepped back outside into the crisp February air, Hannah took a deep breath. One difficult conversation down. One more to go.

Twenty-One

HANNAH

HANNAH PARKED her car in front of the church and sat for a moment, gathering courage. She'd driven past the building twice before finally forcing herself to turn into the parking lot.

The damaged, stained glass window was visible even from here—the century-old window now covered with plywood and plastic sheeting. The sight sent a fresh wave of guilt crashing through her chest.

Hannah switched off the engine and leaned her forehead against the steering wheel. What had possessed her to think that a silly game with Luke and Carter would solve anything? That pretending to be the center of some preposterous romantic triangle would somehow make people forget about that New Year's Eve kiss?

She climbed out of her car, the frigid February air biting at her cheeks as she crossed the parking lot. She forced herself to walk around the side of the building to examine the damage closer, her throat tight.

Tiny shards of colored glass still sparkled on the sidewalk, wedged deep in the cracks of the concrete, stubbornly clinging despite someone's best effort to sweep them away. Each fragment caught the winter sunlight like an accusation.

Hannah hesitated, her breath forming a cloud in the cold air as she tried to gather her thoughts. With a final glance at the broken glass, she turned away and climbed the steps to the front entrance.

The church's wooden door creaked as she pulled it open. Her footsteps echoed on the polished floors as she made her way past the fellowship hall, despite her best efforts not to make a sound.

She expected to encounter Mrs. Peterson bustling about somewhere. The church secretary seemed to materialize whenever anyone entered the building, like she had some kind of sixth sense about visitors. But the hallway remained empty, and Hannah breathed a small sigh of relief.

The door to Ben's office was partially open, and through the gap, she could see him sitting at his desk, a pen moving steadily across a yellow pad of paper. She knocked, her knuckles barely making a sound against the wood.

Ben looked up from his desk, surprise flickering across his face when he spotted her. His expression softened immediately. "Hannah," he said, setting down his pen. "Come in."

"I probably should have called first," she said, lingering near the doorway. "If this is a bad time..."

"Not at all." He gestured to the chair in front of his desk. "Please, sit down. Would you like some coffee? I just made a pot."

Hannah shook her head. She perched on the edge of the chair, back straight, suddenly aware of everything—the gentle tick of the wall clock, the faint smell of his freshly brewed coffee, the way her heart hammered against her ribs. A few personal touches had appeared since the last time she'd been in this office: a framed photograph of Ben, standing on a mountain ledge, a worn leather Bible, a signed Nebraska football helmet.

He pulled up a chair to sit across from her, rather than returning to his desk. The gesture felt significant, as if he was deliberately removing any physical barrier between them.

"I'm so sorry." The words tumbled out in a rush. "For the window. For the Festival ending early, for Luke and Carter…" She paused, forcing herself to slow down. "All of it."

Ben leaned forward slightly, his brown eyes gentle but serious. "You don't owe me an apology, Hannah. Accidents happen."

"This wasn't just an accident," she said. "This was the result of something Luke, Carter, and I started weeks ago. Something that got completely out of hand."

Ben tipped his head, giving her his full attention. "I'm listening."

Hannah watched her fingers twist the strap of her purse. "The dating competition. Wyatt's pool. All of it was fake."

She looked up, forcing herself to meet his eyes. "It was supposed to be harmless. Just a silly distraction to make folks forget about New Year's Eve. But then it got out of hand with the pool and the Festival, and ..." Hannah's words died in her throat.

"I wondered," he said, his expression more thoughtful than angry or shocked. "Carter and Luke both seemed more interested in the competition with each other than in actually dating you. And neither one seemed particularly jealous when you spent time with the other—just eager to plan their next move. To make the next date a little bigger, a little bolder."

His mouth curved into that gentle smile that always made her stomach flutter. "Then, when Wyatt started the Valentine's Day pool, it was obvious that whatever was happening between you three wasn't a typical love triangle."

Hannah felt her cheeks burn hotter. "Well, you won't have to worry about us embarrassing you any more," she said, her voice tight with shame. "It's over. All of it. I told Luke and Carter this morning that this ends today. No more pool. No more silly dates. No more love triangle." She looked down at her hands, unable to meet his eyes.

Ben leaned forward, his elbows on his knees. "Hannah, I never felt embarrassed by you or your friends." He paused, as if trying to decide what to say next. "Confused, sometimes. Amused, often. But never embarrassed."

"You should have been embarrassed," she said, her voice barely above a whisper. "The whole thing was mortifying. Half the town placing bets on my love life. Luke and Carter turning your committee meetings into a—" She stopped, wrapping her arms around herself.

"I think what you three did was brave," Ben said, his voice filled with quiet conviction.

Hannah's head snapped up, her eyes searching his face. "Brave?"

"You and your friends cared about someone else's feelings enough to go to extraordinary lengths to protect him. Even if that someone was me, and even if I didn't need protecting."

The sincerity in his voice made her chest ache. She'd expected judgment, disappointment, maybe even anger. Instead, he was offering her grace she didn't deserve.

"But the window—"

"Will be repaired," he said.

She took another deep breath, steadying herself for the hardest part. "There's something else I have to tell you. Something you most definitely will find embarrassing."

Ben waited, his expression open and patient.

Hannah took a deep breath, taking in that familiar scent of leather and spice she knew would always remind her of him. "Despite everything that has happened since New Year's Eve, despite all the distractions and fake dates and everything Luke and Carter have done to help me move on..." She swallowed hard, her voice dropping to barely a whisper. "I haven't been able to stop thinking about you."

She glanced up, catching a flicker of shock in Ben's eyes before looking away again, focusing on the cross hanging on the wall behind him. It was easier somehow, not looking directly at him while she laid her heart bare. "I know this is completely inappropriate. You're the new pastor. Your reputation in this town, your ability to lead this congregation... that has to be your first priority."

"Hannah—" Ben said, but she held up her hand.

"Please, let me finish. I need to say this." She took a deep breath. "I would never want to become a source of gossip that could undermine your ministry while you're here. I will find another church—at least until Pastor John returns."

"Hannah, that's not—"

"It's okay," she rushed on, the words tumbling out faster now. "I've thought about this. I'll keep my distance, I promise. Eventually, people will forget all of this—the kiss, the competition, the broken window. They'll just see you as Pastor Ben, not..." She swallowed hard. "Not the man I kissed on New Year's Eve."

"Hannah!" Ben's voice was firm, cutting through her frantic words and stopping her cold. "Please. Just listen."

She fell silent, her heart hammering against her ribs.

"First," he said, "I don't want you to find another church. Not unless you want to."

Hannah blinked in surprise. "But—"

"Second," he said, his smile gentle but firm, "As the interim pastor of this church, I'm called to lead a congregation of real people, and that means living a real life. It doesn't mean I have to choose between my ministry and..." He paused, his voice catching slightly. "And the possibility of love."

The word hung in the air between them.

Hannah stared at him, trying to process what he was saying.

Ben's smile deepened, and the dimple Hannah adored appeared in his left cheek. "And since we're being honest with each other, I should tell you I haven't been able to stop thinking about you, either."

Hannah's heart jumped into her throat. "You haven't?"

He nodded. "But as you've pointed out, as the new pastor in town, I wasn't exactly in a position to officially throw my name into the pool to compete for your Valentine's Day date."

Hannah's mouth fell open. She felt dizzy, as if the world had tilted on its axis. "You've been thinking about me?" she asked, hardly daring to believe it.

"Every day," he said simply.

Her breath caught. She could see the sincerity in his brown eyes, and suddenly the walls she'd been trying to build around her heart came tumbling down.

"So what happens now?"

Ben's eyes softened as he looked at her. "Well, that depends. Are you free for supper on Valentine's Day?"

The question hung between them, simple and terrifying and wonderful all at once. She laughed, joy bubbling up from her chest and spilling onto her face. "Yes," she said. "As a matter of fact, I am. My calendar just opened up this morning."

Twenty-Two

BEN

BEN STARED at the blank page before him, the words refusing to flow. An open Bible lay beside his legal pad, several verses highlighted but none speaking to him with the clarity he needed. Two hours of work, and all he had to show for it was a wastebasket overflowing with discarded ideas and a growing headache behind his eyes.

Through his office window, the afternoon sun cast long shadows across the church lawn. In just over twenty-four hours, he would pick Hannah up for their date. His stomach tightened with a mixture of anticipation and anxiety that made sermon-writing nearly impossible.

Ben rubbed his temples, trying to ease the tension gathering there. It had been two days since Hannah had stood in his office, brave and trembling, and he still hadn't stopped replaying the moment. He hadn't planned on asking her out. Well, not while he was still the pastor at her church, anyway. But sitting across from her, hearing her admit to having feelings for him, seeing the vulnerability in her expression, the words had simply tumbled out: "Are you free for supper on Valentine's Day?"

Ben turned back to his notes, forcing himself to focus on Ecclesiastes 4: 9-12. *Two are better than one, because they have a good return for their labor: if either of them falls down, one can help the other up.* The verse had seemed perfect when he'd picked it out, offering the perfect foundation for a sermon about community and connection. Instead, Ben found himself fixating on the implication of partnership, of two people choosing to walk through life side by side.

He groaned in frustration and crumpled the page, tossing it toward the wastebasket. It hit the rim and bounced across the floor, rolling to a stop near the door. Yet another failure in an afternoon full of them.

As he pushed back his chair and stood to retrieve it, his phone rang. The sudden sound in the quiet office made him jump. He glanced at the screen, and his stomach dropped.

Pastor John Harrison.

Ben stared at the name, a cold wave of apprehension washing over him. Had someone told Pastor John about his date with Hannah? Bluestem was a small town, and news traveled fast. What if someone had called to complain about the interim pastor dating a parishioner?

The phone continued to ring, demanding an answer.

He took a deep breath, steadying himself. Whatever Pastor John had to say, Ben would listen. He would explain his feelings for Hannah honestly and accept whatever guidance the older pastor offered. He had too much respect both for Pastor John and his own calling to do otherwise.

With that resolution, Ben picked up the phone before it went to voicemail. He cleared his throat, willing his voice to sound normal. "Pastor Ben speaking."

"Don't sound so formal, Ben. It's me, Pastor John. How's Bluestem treating you? Mrs. Peterson keeping you well-supplied with those lemon bars of hers?"

Ben exhaled slowly, his shoulders relaxing as he settled back into his chair. "She is, though I might need new pants by the time you get back."

"That woman's baking is both a blessing and a trial," Pastor John said, laughing. "How's everything else going? Church running smoothly?"

The older pastor's easy laughter chased away all traces of Ben's anxiety. "As well as can be expected," he said, twirling a pen between his fingers. "Though we did have a minor incident at the Winter Festival. A broken stained glass window during a snowball fight."

"Ah, yes. Mrs. Peterson mentioned that in her weekly update email."

Ben smiled, picturing Pastor John receiving detailed weekly reports from Mrs. Peterson while he recovered. "How's the knee? Making progress?"

"That's actually why I'm calling." Pastor John's voice took on a more serious tone. "Physical therapy's going well, but my doctor and I have been having some long conversations about my future. About what's realistic at my age."

Ben straightened in his chair, sensing a shift in the conversation. "What do you mean?"

Pastor John sighed. "I've decided to retire, Ben. My doctor thinks it's time, and after praying about it, I do too. Thirty-seven years in ministry is enough for any man, and these old bones are telling me it's time to enjoy my grandkids while I can still chase them around—even if it's with a slight limp."

"Retire?" Ben repeated, the word hanging in the air between them. "Are you sure? I know how much you love this congregation."

"That I do," Pastor John said, his voice warm with affection. "Which is why I wanted to talk to you directly. The church council has been extremely impressed with your leadership. Your sermons, your pastoral care, the way you handled the whole Winter Festival mishap. They'd like to offer you the permanent position, if you're interested."

Ben gripped the edge of his desk, steadying himself against the wave of surprise. "The permanent position," he echoed, struggling to process the implications. "Pastor John, I don't know what to say. I wasn't planning on this."

"I know," Pastor John said. "And you don't

need to decide this minute." He paused, then added, "Is there anything that might hold you back from accepting? Bluestem's a small town, but it's a special place. A good place to put down roots."

Ben's thoughts immediately turned to Hannah.

"There is something," Ben admitted, his voice dropping lower, even though he was alone in his office. "Someone, actually."

"Ah," Pastor John said, and Ben could almost hear the smile in his voice. "Would this someone be a certain redheaded newspaper employee who chairs the Winter Festival committee?"

Heat crept up Ben's neck. "How did you—"

"Mrs. Peterson is a very observant woman. She overhead you make a reservation in Valentine for Valentine's Day, and put two and two together. She thought it was very romantic, by the way."

Ben ran a hand through his hair, unsure whether to be mortified or relieved. "I should have expected that," he said. "There are no secrets in Bluestem, are there?"

"No, not really. But dating Hannah doesn't

have to be a secret, you know. Ministry isn't meant to be a solitary journey, Ben. God calls us to serve, yes, but not at the expense of the very human connections that enrich our understanding of divine love."

Pastor John's voice softened, and Ben could picture him leaning forward in his chair, as if they were sitting in the same room. "Will there be challenges? Of course. Some folks will gossip. But in my experience, congregations are remarkably supportive of a pastor's happiness, provided he remains devoted to his calling."

Ben felt something tight in his chest loosen. "So you think it's possible to be both—a good pastor and a man pursuing a relationship?"

"Not just possible—preferable," Pastor John said firmly. "The best pastors I know have strong partnerships that ground them. Besides, Hannah Mitchell is one of the finest young women in this town. Kind, faithful, active in the church and community. She's exactly the kind of person who understands the demands of ministry."

He paused and cleared his throat. "Ben, you have two blessings before you—a congregation that needs a shepherd and a woman who might be your perfect partner. I can't tell you what to decide, but I can tell you I'd be honored to know you were following me in both the pulpit and in discovering the joy this community can bring."

Ben swallowed hard, unexpected emotion tightening his throat. "Thank you," he said. "I really needed to hear those words, right now."

When the call ended, Ben set the phone down carefully. The office felt different somehow—bigger, filled with possibilities he hadn't allowed himself to consider until now. He returned to his desk and pulled out a fresh sheet of paper. Suddenly, the sermon that had eluded him all afternoon seemed clear. *Two are better than one, because they have a good return for their labor.* It wasn't just about romantic partnerships, but about all the ways humans support and strengthen each other—through friendship, through community, through faith.

As Ben wrote, the words flowed easily from his pen, filling the page with a clarity that had eluded him all day. He paused, watching the late afternoon sunlight slant through his office window, casting long shadows across the desk. A sense of peace settled over him. Whatever path opened before him—with Hannah, with the church, with this small town that was beginning to feel like home—he would walk it with confidence, trusting the Lord to guide his every step.

Twenty-Three

HANNAH

HANNAH STARED AT HER REFLECTION. The harsh bathroom lights turned her hair the color of a polished penny. She tucked a curl behind her ear, then untucked it, then tried to tame it with a spritz of hairspray before giving up and letting it spring free again. There was no winning a battle with the Mitchell family hair—only temporary truces.

Her deep red sweater hugged her shoulders and complemented the green in her eyes; at least, that's what Alyssa had told her when she'd bought it, which was exactly why she'd chosen it, but now she was second-guessing everything. Maybe it was too much? She'd already cycled through three different outfits and her bedroom looked like a department store fitting room after Black Friday.

She checked her watch for the eighth time in as many minutes. 5:23. Ben said he'd pick her up at 5:30, which meant she still had seven minutes to either calm down or spiral into a complete panic. She smoothed the front of her sweater, then checked her teeth in the mirror, then debated whether she should switch from boots to flats.

She moved to her dresser, opening her jewelry box and considering her options. Too much would seem like she was trying too hard. Too little might suggest she didn't care enough. Finally, she settled on the simple silver snowflake necklace her parents had given her for Christmas—understated but pretty, catching the light just right.

Her hands trembled slightly as she fastened the clasp, and she took a deep breath. "Get it together, Hannah," she murmured to her reflection. "It's just dinner."

But it wasn't just dinner. It was a real Valentine's date with Ben. A date with the man who—

against all odds—wanted to go out with her, Hannah Mitchell, the woman who'd caused him nothing but trouble since he'd arrived in Bluestem.

"I haven't been able to stop thinking about you, either," he'd said. The memory of those words sent a deep, hopeful warmth curling through her stomach. She headed downstairs to her living room and its big picture window, peering through the curtains at her empty driveway. No sign of Ben's Jeep Wrangler yet.

She took a deep breath, straightened her shoulders, and gave herself a silent pep talk. This was Ben. Pastor Ben. There was no reason to be nervous.

Except, of course, for the minor detail that her heart had been doing somersaults ever since he'd asked her out.

Her phone buzzed in her purse. She picked it up to find a text from Alyssa:

> Good luck tonight! Call me
> tomorrow with ALL the
> details. xo

Hannah smiled, remembering Alyssa's

excited squeal when she'd shared the news about her date with Ben. Riley had overheard, of course, and by lunchtime, Luke and Carter knew as well.

LUKE

About time. I was running out of romantic gestures.

Another buzz of her phone. This time it was Carter.

Don't let the good pastor bore you to death with theology. If he does, text us and Luke and I will stage a rescue mission.

The sound of an engine pulled her from her thoughts. Hannah's heart leaped into her throat as she rushed back to the window. Ben's black Jeep was pulling into her driveway, its headlights sweeping across her front porch.

She watched as he emerged from the car, tall and solid in his charcoal gray coat and matching Stetson. Hannah took one last look at herself in the hall mirror, smoothed her hair, and waited for the doorbell to ring. When it did, she counted to three before opening the door, not wanting to appear as if she'd been waiting by the window like an eager teenager.

Ben smiled when he saw her, his dimple in full view, and Hannah felt that now-familiar flutter in her chest again.

"Hello, Pastor Ben," she said, immediately regretting how formal it sounded.

Ben's smile widened. "Just Ben. No pastoral duties tonight. Just a regular guy taking the most popular woman in Bluestem out on Valentine's Night."

Hannah laughed, the sound coming out a little breathless. "You've been talking to Lenny Beckett, I see."

Ben chuckled, a rich sound that seemed to wrap around her. "Mrs. Peterson—who apparently heard it from Lenny Beckett."

She grabbed her coat from the hook by the door, and Ben immediately stepped forward to help her into it, his hands resting lightly on her shoulders as she slipped her arms through the sleeves. The gesture was old-fashioned but charming, reminding Hannah of the way her father still helped her mother with her coat on the rare occasions they went out to dinner.

Outside, the February air was crisp and cold, their breath forming small clouds between them as Ben guided her to the passenger side of his car.

"I hope you don't mind," he said as he started the engine, "but I made reservations at a steakhouse in Valentine. The perfect place for a Valentine's Night date, I thought."

Hannah turned to look at him, surprised. Valentine was forty-five miles away—far enough that their first real date wouldn't be the main topic of conversation tomorrow morning at Daisy's Diner or the Rusty Spur.

The thoughtfulness behind his choice touched her deeply. "That sounds perfect," she said, and meant it. The tension she'd been carrying in her shoulders eased as they left the familiar streets of her neighborhood behind. "I have to admit, the idea of eating dinner without wondering who is watching is pretty appealing."

Ben chuckled, the sound low and warm in the quiet car. "I figured as much. Besides, I've been wanting to try this place since I moved to Bluestem. Clayton Leisiak raves about their steaks, and Mrs. Peterson said to be sure to order the bread pudding for dessert."

Halfway to Valentine, Ben reached over, palm up on the center console. Hannah hesitated, then placed her hand in his. Their fingers laced together naturally.

"So," Ben said, glancing at her with a smile that made her toes curl inside her boots, "tell me about your day."

Twenty-Four

HANNAH

THE LONGVIEW STEAKHOUSE stood at the edge of town, a sprawling log cabin with warm golden light spilling from every window. As Ben held the door open for her, Hannah stepped into a world of rustic charm: exposed wooden beams crossed the ceiling, iron chandeliers cast a soft light over the dining area, and the scent of grilled meat and freshly baked bread wrapped around her like a warm embrace.

"Happy Valentine's Day," a young hostess greeted them, her smile bright and professional. "Do you have a reservation?"

"Yes. Landry, party of two."

The hostess checked her book and nodded. "Right this way, please."

She brought them to a corner booth, partially hidden by a stone fireplace that crackled with a low flame. "Your server will be with you shortly," she said, handing them each a leather-bound menu before departing.

Hannah slid into the booth, appreciating the privacy the corner location gave them. From here, they could see most of the restaurant, but few people could see them. It felt like their own little world, insulated from prying eyes and curious glances.

Hannah shrugged off her coat, suddenly aware of how intimate this felt. Just Ben and her, no audience, no distractions.

They ordered—wine, salad, steak and potatoes, with bread pudding for dessert. Ben told stories about his childhood in North Dakota, about his mother's relentless optimism and his dad's devotion to fixing up old cars. Hannah shared stories about her siblings, the controlled chaos of growing up in a house with five kids and a mom who believed in the healing power of homemade soup.

"You're smiling," Ben said. "What are you thinking about?"

"How nice this is," she said, surprised by the contentment she heard in her own voice.

"It is," Ben said, his voice carrying a similar note of contentment. "No committees to run, no festivals to plan, no broken windows to worry about."

Hannah laughed, the sound lighter than it had been in days. "No betting pools, no fake competitions, no snowball fights."

"Just dinner," Ben said, glancing over at her with a smile that made her heart skip. "Just us."

The drive back to Bluestem passed in a comfortable blend of conversation and companionable silence. When Ben pulled into her driveway, Hannah felt a flutter of disappointment. The evening had been wonderful, and she wasn't ready for it to end.

Ben shifted the Jeep into park but left the engine running, warm air still flowing from the vents.

"Thank you for dinner," she said, turning to face him. "It was a perfect first date."

"It was," Ben agreed, his voice soft in the quiet space between them. He glanced toward her house, then back at her, something uncertain flickering in his expression.

"Would you like to come in for coffee?" she asked, then immediately second-guessed herself. Was that too forward? Too presumptuous?

Ben's smile was gentle. "I'd like that, but…" He glanced toward her house, then back at her. "Maybe we could sit outside for a while instead? I know it's cold, but it's a beautiful night."

Hannah followed his gaze to her front porch, to the old wooden swing. She'd inherited the swing from the previous owners, along with a weathered storage box where she kept quilted blankets.

"I'd like that," Hannah said, surprised by how much she meant it.

Ben came around to open her door, offering his hand to help her out. The chilly February air hit Hannah's face as she stepped out of the warmth of Ben's car, but she didn't mind. Her hand felt cozy and safe in his as they walked up the cement path to her small front porch.

Hannah lifted the lid of the storage box and pulled out two old quilts. She spread one on the bench and gestured for Ben to have a seat. She settled beside him on the swing, then unfolded the second quilt and draped it across their laps. The wooden seat creaked softly under their combined weight as Ben pushed gently with his feet, setting them into a slow, rhythmic motion.

For a few minutes, they simply swayed gently. Hannah felt perfectly content to stay like this, wrapped in warmth and silence and the growing certainty that something significant was happening between them.

Ben was the first to break the silence. "Hannah, there's something I need to talk to you about. Something I've been waiting for the right moment to say."

Hannah's stomach tightened at the serious note in his voice. Her contentment suddenly felt fragile, like a soap bubble that might pop at the slightest touch. She turned to look at him, searching his face in the soft glow of the porch light.

He took her hands in his, his fingers warm despite the chilly night air. "Pastor John called me yesterday," Ben said, his grip on her hands tightening slightly. "He's decided to retire. The church council met this morning. They've offered me a permanent position."

The words hung in the air between them. Her hands went cold in his warm grasp, and her heart stuttered to what felt like a complete stop before hammering back to life with a vengeance. If Ben accepted, he would be their pastor. Her pastor. For real.

"What did you tell them?" she asked.

"I told them I needed to think about it. Talk it over with... someone important to me." His brown eyes held hers steadily. "Dating as a pastor comes with certain... challenges," he said carefully. He didn't look away from her, but she sensed him choosing his words carefully, like someone navigating a minefield. "Especially when that person is a member of his congregation."

"I know," she said. "People will talk."

Ben nodded, his thumbs tracing gentle circles across her knuckles. "They will," he said. "About you. About me. About whether I'm letting personal feelings influence church decisions." He leaned forward slightly. "I don't want you to be blindsided by any of that."

Hannah felt her heart sink even as she tried to keep her expression neutral. The words hit her like a physical blow as the full meaning of what

Ben was telling her sank in. He wasn't asking for her blessing to accept the position—he was preparing her for why they couldn't be together if he did.

Hannah took a shaky breath, the cold air burning her lungs. "I understand," she said, proud that her voice came out steady despite the way her heart was cracking apart in her chest. "They need to see you as someone who puts the church first. Not someone who's... who's distracted by—"

Ben's grip on her hands tightened. "Hannah—"

"No, it's okay. I get it. People need to get to know you and trust you as their pastor."

"Hannah, please—" Ben started again, his voice more urgent now.

"You're right. We need to stop now. Before this gets any more complicated. Dating me will just make your job harder."

"Hannah, look at me."

She forced herself to meet his gaze, expecting to see sympathy or gentle rejection or frustration. Instead, she found something else entirely—a quiet determination that made her pulse quicken.

"I'm not saying we shouldn't date," he said. "I'm saying we should be prepared for what will happen if we do." Ben's eyes searched her face. "I want you to know that I've prayed about this. About us. About what it means to serve a congregation while having romantic feelings for someone within it."

His voice dropped lower, more intimate. "And I keep coming back to the same conclusion. Spending time with you won't make me a worse pastor. It will make me a better one." Ben shifted on the swing, angling his body toward her more fully.

"What exactly are you saying?" Hannah asked, her voice barely above a whisper.

Ben took a deep breath. "What I'm trying to say is… if you're willing to give this a shot, I'd like to stay. I'd like to accept the church's offer and keep building something here—with the church *and* with you. But only if *you're* comfortable with what that means. Because it might not be easy."

Hannah's heart hammered against her ribs as she processed his words. Then she nodded. "I want that too," she said, the words coming out in a whisper before she could change her mind.

Ben's smile was radiant, his dimple deepening as relief washed over his features. He lifted her hand to his lips and pressed a gentle kiss to her knuckles, the warmth of his breath sending shivers up her arm. "Really?" he asked, and she could hear the wonder in his voice, as if he'd been bracing himself for a different answer.

"Really," she said, laughing at his expression. "Though I have to warn you—dating me comes with its own set of challenges. I have a proven track record of making things very awkward, very quickly."

He squeezed her hand, his eyes filled with laughter. "Good. I like awkward. Especially if it ends in a kiss."

The words hung between them in the frigid air, and Hannah felt her breath catch in her throat. "How do you know my awkward moments end in kisses?" she asked.

"Well," Ben said, his voice dropping to a low, intimate tone that made her heart beat faster. "I have some experience with that. New Year's Eve being a prime example."

The memory of their kiss rushed back with startling clarity: the warmth of his hands at her waist, the look of bewilderment in his eyes, the way his lips had felt on hers.

"And speaking of kisses," Ben continued, his thumbs once again tracing gentle circles across her knuckles, "I've been thinking we should do it again."

Hannah's pulse skittered at his words, heat blooming in her cheeks despite the cold air. "That sounds like an excellent idea."

"Good," he said. "Because I've been thinking about kissing you every day for the past six weeks." His smile deepened, and he shifted closer on the bench swing. His hands came up to cup her cheeks, his thumbs brushing across her lips with the same gentle reverence he'd shown her hands.

When he leaned down to kiss her, Hannah felt the rest of the world fade away. This wasn't the impulsive, cider-flavored kiss of New Year's Eve—this was deliberate, tender, full of promise. Ben's lips were warm despite the wintry air, and his hands were gentle. She could feel his heartbeat through his coat where her palms rested against his chest, could hear the soft creak of the porch swing, could taste the lingering sweetness of the wine they'd shared at dinner.

When they broke apart, Hannah felt breathless. Ben rested his forehead against hers, his breath forming small puffs in the frigid air between them.

"Better than I remembered," he said.

"Much better."

They sat there for a moment, wrapped in the peaceful silence of the quiet night. The February air swirled around them, but Hannah barely noticed it, wrapped as she was in Ben's arms and the glow of something new and real beginning between them.

"So what happens next?" she asked, tilting her head to look up at him. The porch light caught the planes of his face, casting gentle shadows that made him look both familiar and mysterious.

Ben's smile was soft in the porch light, his thumb tracing gentle patterns across her cheek. "First, I call the church council and accept their offer," he said. "Then I take you on another date. And another one after that, if you'll have me."

Hannah laughed, joy bubbling up in her chest. After weeks of pretending and schemes and over-the-top gestures, the simplicity of his words felt endearingly perfect. "I think I can manage that."

He leaned down and kissed her again,

tenderly. "Happy Valentine's Day, Hannah," he murmured against her lips.

Her smile deepened, her heart lighter than it had been in weeks. "Happy Valentine's Day, Ben."

Epilogue

HANNAH

New Year's Eve

Hannah checked her reflection in the hallway mirror again. She had on a shimmery blue top, warm black leggings, and her favorite pair of boots. She smiled. Alyssa was right. It was the perfect outfit for Wyatt's annual New Year's Eve party at the Rusty Spur.

Through her picture window, she could see snow falling in thick, lazy flakes, coating the porch railings and the bare branches of the oak tree in her front yard. The Christmas lights Ben had helped her string around the porch last month twinkled through the snow, casting a warm glow that made everything look like a scene from a holiday card.

One year. That's how long it had been since that impulsive kiss under the mistletoe. A year of quiet dinners and long conversations, of Ben holding her hand during movies and Hannah helping him grade confirmation class assignments. A year of learning how to navigate the gentle gossip and veiled warnings from well-meaning but nosy neighbors, and figuring out that most of the congregation was more interested in keeping Ben in Bluestem for as long as possible than in any imagined scandal.

The sound of tires crunching on her ice and snow-covered driveway pulled her from her thoughts. She watched through the window as Ben emerged from his Jeep, tall and steady in his signature charcoal coat and gray Stetson. Snow dusted his shoulders as he made his way up the walkway, and Hannah felt that same flutter of anticipation in her chest that had become so familiar, yet no less thrilling, over the past year.

She opened the door before he could knock. "Right on time," she said, smiling up at him.

"I try to be," Ben said, his dimple deepening as he grinned, "unlike my beautiful girlfriend."

The snowflakes in his hair glittered under the porch light, and Hannah fought the urge to reach up and brush them away. Instead, she laughed and pulled him inside. "I was ready early tonight, thank you very much." She reached for her cream-colored scarf. "Do you think it'll still be snowing at midnight?"

Ben helped her with her coat, his hands lingering at her shoulders. "I hope so. There's something magical about starting a new year with snow falling." He paused, then added, "You know, it's such a beautiful night. What do you say we walk to the Rusty Spur? It's only a few blocks."

Hannah glanced out at the gently falling snow. "Walk? In this?"

"Please? I think you'll be glad we did."

Something in his tone made her curious. There was a hint of something in his eyes— something like anticipation mixed with nervousness. "All right," she said, wrapping her scarf more securely around her neck. "But if my toes freeze, I'm holding you personally responsible."

Ben laughed, the sound rich and deep. "You can warm them up dancing."

"I thought you didn't like to dance," Hannah said, giving him a teasing look.

"I like it," he said, adjusting his hat. "I'm just not very good at it. But rumor has it, Carter and Luke are both flying solo again to the party this year."

Hannah's smile widened as she buttoned up her coat. "You're not getting out of dancing with me that easily, Pastor Landry."

They stepped out into the night, the snow crunching beneath their boots. Ben took her hand and tucked it into the crook of his arm as they made their way down the street, the twinkling holiday decorations casting a magical glow over everything.

"This was a good idea," Hannah said as they walked. "It *is* beautiful out here."

"I thought we might take the scenic route," Ben said, guiding her toward the town square.

"The scenic route? Ben Landry, what are you up to?"

His only answer was a squeeze of her hand.

As they approached the town square, Hannah could see that someone had strung additional lights around the gazebo. They twinkled like stars against the night sky, reflecting off the fresh snow.

"Oh, Ben, look at the gazebo! It's beautiful," Hannah said, tugging him toward it.

"I thought you might say that," he said, following her lead as she pulled him up the steps and into the shelter of the white wooden structure.

Inside, the old wooden bench had been cleared of snow and decorated with a small arrangement of holly berries. The "hitching bench." The same bench Carter had dubbed "the bench of no return".

"Ben?" she questioned, turning to find him watching her with an intensity that made her breath catch. His hand disappeared into his coat pocket, and for a wild, heart-stopping moment, Hannah thought he was going to propose. Instead, he pulled out a sprig of mistletoe, its white berries glistening in the twinkling lights.

He tucked the mistletoe into the rafters above them. "I thought maybe we should practice before we get to Wyatt's. Make sure we're ready for midnight."

Hannah laughed. "Practice does make perfect," she said, stepping into the circle of his arms.

But instead of drawing her close for a kiss,

Ben took a small step back. His expression shifted, something deeper replacing the playful glint in his eyes. "Hannah," he said, his voice lower now, more deliberate. "I've been thinking about last New Year's Eve a lot lately."

He paused, and she gave him a questioning look. She'd never quite figured out how to read his silences, even after a year together.

"That kiss changed everything," he said, his eyes never leaving hers. "One impulsive moment that altered the course of both of our lives." He reached back into his coat pocket, and this time, withdrew a small velvet box, deep blue against his palm.

Hannah felt her lips part in surprise, her eyes widening as the full realization of what was happening washed over her.

"Ben," she whispered, her voice barely audible over the sudden rush of blood in her ears.

Ben's smile was tender as he looked at her. "Last year, you kissed me on impulse," he said, opening the box to reveal a delicate ring. One large diamond caught the light, flanked by smaller diamonds that glittered like the snow.

"Now, and for the rest of my life, I want to kiss you on purpose."

Tears welled in Hannah's eyes, blurring her vision as Ben continued, his voice steady despite the emotion that made it deeper than usual.

"I love you, Hannah Mitchell. I love your impulsiveness and your kindness. I love how you care for this town and the people in it. I love watching you organize festivals and fall asleep during movie nights." He took her hands, his thumbs brushing across her knuckles in that familiar, comforting way. "I want to spend every day learning more about you, growing with you, serving alongside you."

A tear slipped down Hannah's cheek as Ben lowered himself to one knee, still holding her hands in his.

"Hannah Mitchell, will you marry me?"

For a moment, Hannah couldn't speak. Her heart seemed to expand in her chest, filling with a joy so complete it left no room for doubt or fear. Her mind flashed through moments from their year together — Ben's laughter as they tried and failed to bake bread during a cooking class at church, his steady hand guiding hers as they carved pumpkins in October, working together to decorate her house for Christmas.

"Yes," she finally managed, her voice breaking on the word. "Yes, Ben. Of course, yes."

Ben's face broke into that radiant smile she loved. He slipped the ring onto her finger—a perfect fit—before rising to his feet and drawing her into his arms.

"I love you," Hannah whispered against his coat, breathing in the familiar scent of leather and spice.

"I love you, too," Ben said, his voice thick with emotion. He cupped her face in his hands, thumbs gently brushing away her tears. Then he glanced up at the mistletoe above them and smiled. "Now, about that practice..."

THE RUSTY SPUR was alive with celebration, golden light spilling from the windows into the snowy night. Hannah could hear the music and laughter even before Ben pulled open the door; the familiar sounds of family and friends gathered to ring in the new year. Colorful streamers in silver and gold hung from the exposed wooden beams, and someone, probably Mrs. K., had draped twinkling lights around the bar and along the windows, casting everything in a warm, festive glow.

"Hannah! Ben!" Alyssa called, weaving through the crowd with Riley close behind. Her friend's sharp eyes went immediately to Hannah's left hand, then let out a shriek loud enough to make the whole bar turn to look. "He did it! Riley, look!"

Hannah barely had time to brace herself before Alyssa enveloped her in a tight hug. "I'm so happy for you," Alyssa whispered fiercely in her ear.

"You knew?" Hannah asked as they pulled apart.

"Ben asked Riley for advice on the ring," Alyssa said with a grin. "And I may have offered some opinions."

Ben laughed, accepting Riley's congratulatory handshake. "More than some," he said, raising an eyebrow at Alyssa. "She had very specific thoughts about cut and setting."

The next few hours blurred into a parade of hugs, handshakes, and toasts. Soon it felt like everyone in Bluestem had joined them at the Spur or was texting congratulations.

At one point, her entire family showed up. There was a chorus of whoops and hollers and oohs and aahs over the ring, followed by her mother's tears and her dad's enormous, wordless hug.

Her youngest sister held her phone out in front of her, live-streaming the entire event for their grandmother. "She says you're not allowed to elope, and she wants at least one dance with the 'hunk'. I assume she's talking about Ben, but with Grandma, she could be talking about Luke or Carter!"

Hannah laughed until her sides ached. Before she knew it, it was eleven-thirty. She leaned back against the padded bench at their table and let herself breathe. Her feet ached, but she didn't mind. Ben had gone to fetch them a couple of sliders and some fries, leaving her with a half-empty glass of diet pop and the steady pulse of the music for company.

"Here you are! We hear 'Congratulations' are in order," Carter said. He slid into the booth across from her with a tray of plastic champagne flutes, followed by Luke, who balanced a bowl of popcorn in one hand and a bottle of sparkling cider in the other.

Luke poured three glasses, handing one to Carter and then one to Hannah. "To you and Ben," he said, clinking his glass against hers. "May the upcoming year be less chaotic than this one."

"Speak for yourself," Carter said, elbowing him. "I expect at least a wedding, a barn dance, and maybe a baby or two before next New Year's Eve."

"A baby or two?" Hannah choked, nearly sputtering bubbles up her nose. "We just got engaged."

Carter leaned back in his seat, a teasing grin spreading across his face as he raised an eyebrow at Hannah. "Ben baptizes babies, doesn't he? What did you think I was talking about, Mitchell?"

Luke glanced at his watch, then back at Hannah with a grin that was pure impishness. "Would you look at the time!" he said. "It's almost midnight."

"So, Mitchell," Carter said, his familiar swagger back in full force as he leaned closer, "who's getting your midnight kiss *this* year?

Luke and I have been dreaming about that kiss ever since we missed out last year." His deadpan delivery made Hannah laugh out loud.

"You're both impossible," she said, her voice warm with affection.

"That's why you love us," Luke said.

Ben rejoined the table, sliding an arm around Hannah's shoulder. "What are you three up to now?" he asked.

"Your fiancée was just agreeing to meet us under the mistletoe at midnight," Carter said, his grin widening at Ben's raised eyebrows. "For old times' sake."

"Is that so?" Ben asked, his voice warm with amusement as he glanced down at Hannah.

Hannah leaned into his side and smiled. "Don't worry," she said. "I've learned my lesson about impulsive kisses under the mistletoe."

"Have you?" Ben asked. "That's a shame. I was rather fond of that one particular impulse." Ben's eyes sparkled as he fished something from the inside pocket of his coat—another sprig of mistletoe. He reached up and hung it above their heads.

Carter and Luke burst out laughing, the

sound blending with the music and the hum of conversation around them.

"Five minutes to midnight, folks!" Wyatt's voice boomed through the speakers, cutting through the New Year's noise. "Grab your drink and someone to kiss—it's almost time!"

Carter winked at Hannah. "Last chance to reconsider your options, Mitchell."

Luke nodded solemnly. "Once that man puts a wedding band on your finger, my lips are off-limits."

Ben drew Hannah closer to his side. His smile was warm, and there was a gleam in his eyes that made Hannah's heart beat faster. "I think it's time for you two men to go find your own gals to kiss," he said, his voice full of patient amusement. "This one's taken."

The look of mock outrage on Carter's face was almost comical. "Is that a challenge, Pastor?"

"More like a fact," Ben said, his smile deepening as he looked down at Hannah. "Permanent and non-negotiable."

"Ten!" Wyatt's voice called out, starting the countdown that was immediately taken up by the crowd. "Nine! Eight! Seven!"

Ben turned to face Hannah fully, both hands coming to rest at her waist. His eyes held hers as the voices around them grew louder.

"Six! Five! Four!"

Carter and Luke slid out of the booth and joined the circle of family and friends that had formed around Hannah and Ben. Alyssa, standing next to Riley, caught Hannah's eye and gave her a thumbs-up, her smile bright with shared joy.

"Three! Two! One! Happy New Year!"

The room erupted in celebration—champagne glasses clinked, noisemakers blared, confetti rained down like colorful snow. But Hannah was only aware of Ben's lips finding hers, warm and sure and full of promise.

"Happy New Year, my soon-to-be Mrs. Landry," Ben whispered, his thumbs brushing gently across her cheekbones.

"Happy New Year, Ben," she whispered back, leaning in to kiss him again as their friends and neighbors celebrated around them and the clock struck twelve on the first day of the rest of their lives.

Is this your first visit to Bluestem?

You can read the "Journey to Bluestem" Series in any order—but if you'd like more time with Hannah and her friends, check out the two books below.

Wrong Wedding Right Guy (Book 1)

A wedding singer, a best man, and one unforgettable duet that hits all the right notes.

Falling for the Rodeo Cowboy (Book 2)

A big-city journalist, a small-town cowboy, and one assignment that puts both their hearts on the line.

Loved your journey to Bluestem?

If you enjoyed your visit to Bluestem and **Winning Hannah's Heart** touched your heart, please take a moment to leave a short review.

Your review helps other readers discover these clean, heartwarming stories and keeps the Bluestem series growing. Even a few words make a big difference.

Join JoAnn's Dream Team at www.JoAnn Charles.com/free and be the first to know when one of her novels is being released!

JoAnn Charles writes clean, heartwarming romantic novels filled with small-town charm, hope, and happily-ever-afters. Her Bluestem cozy stories celebrate love, laughter, and the power of community, set in a place where everyone knows your name and second chances are always on the menu.

When she's not writing about love in Bluestem, JoAnn can be found enjoying coffee with friends, dreaming up her next story, or spending time with her family.

She also writes children's books under the pen name **N. L. Sharp**.